Prais

EMI
SHAD

'A wonderfully imaginative tale about the power of sisterly love and defying the entangled threads of fate'
Andy Sagar, author of *Yesterday Crumb and the Storm in a Teacup*

'Rebecca King has written an exceptional compelling debut – another star in the making for UK children's literature'
Alex Wheatle, author of *Crongton Knights*

'Such fun, fizzing with ideas and a great, really original adventure'
Penny Chrimes, author of *Tiger Heart*

'Thrilling, filled with memorable images and shot through with the delicious dream logic of Lewis Carroll and Norton Juster'
Mark Powers, author of *Space Detectives*

'Rebecca King has created something really special . . . it is fabulous'
Justine Windsor, author of *Goodly and Grave*

ALSO BY REBECCA KING

Ember Shadows and the Fates of Mount Never

REBECCA KING

EMBER SHADOWS

and the LOST DESERT of TIME

Orion

ORION CHILDREN'S BOOKS

First published in Great Britain in 2023
by Hodder & Stoughton

1 3 5 7 9 10 8 6 4 2

A CIP catalogue record for this book
is available from the British Library.

ISBN 978 1 51011 003 8

Typeset in Sabon by Avon DataSet Ltd, Alcester, Warwickshire

Printed and bound in Great Britain by Clays Ltd, Elcograf S.p.A.

The paper and board used in this book are made
from wood from responsible sources.

Orion Children's Books
An imprint of
Hachette Children's Group
Part of Hodder & Stoughton Limited
Carmelite House
50 Victoria Embankment
London EC4Y 0DZ

An Hachette UK Company
www.hachette.co.uk

www.hachettechildrens.co.uk

To my parents
My mum, who makes me feel as though
I can do anything.
And my dad, who never lets me give up.

1

The two girls crouched at the edge of the forest, their shadows stretching out ahead of them in the moonlight.

Heads close together, they stared at a map unfurled on the grass. Ember, the eldest, pushed her auburn hair behind her ears and looked at her sister.

'It's up to you, Juniper,' she said. Excitement shone from her eyes. 'Which way?'

Juniper bit her lip and studied the map some more. 'It's so hard, there are so many tunnels,' she said.

Ember grinned. There *were* a lot of tunnels, which meant a *lot* of exploring to do. She looked up at the enormous mountain towering overhead. Light from the stars seemed to bounce off it, making it glitter.

Mount Never.

She turned back to Juniper, who was still poring over the mountain's map. 'Come on,' Ember said, nudging her sister. 'We'll explore them all eventually. You just need to choose one for your first adventure.'

Juniper nodded and pointed at a long black line on the map. 'That one,' she said.

'Let's go, then!' Ember said, standing and holding her hand out.

Juniper didn't take it, but smiled, and began to make her way towards the mountain alone.

With a roll of her eyes, Ember gathered up the map and followed. Juniper was desperate to appear grown up, despite only being eight years old. Still, Ember would be right there to protect her if she needed it, though thankfully the most dangerous thing on the mountain had been gone for weeks.

They arrived at the foot of Mount Never together, pausing in front of an iron arch, the mountain's name twisted into the frame like vines.

'HEY!' shouted a voice from behind them. 'Wait for me!' it called.

The sisters turned back towards their village to see a small metallic object bouncing towards them. In the moonlight, only its clock-hand-shaped body was visible. Still, Ember would have known her best friend anywhere.

'Hans!' she said.

As he approached them, hopping above the grass, Ember could make out more of his features. His little hands waved frantically and his toothy grin beamed up at her. Even after sharing a magical adventure together, Ember still found it incredible to think that she had a talking clock hand as a friend.

'Were you going on an adventure without me?' asked Hans with a pout, his turned-out feet landing on the ground in front of them.

'You said you were too busy playing chess against yourself to come, no matter *what* we were doing,' Ember reminded him.

'Well, I won!' Hans said, gleefully clapping his hands together. 'So, now that I'm victorious, where are we going? To lands unknown? Mystical and magical and marvellous and—'

'Not exactly,' interrupted Ember, knowing Hans could go on for a *long* time once he got started. 'We're going *inside* Mount Never.'

'Inside?' he asked, eyes lighting up.

'Yes. And actually, the tunnel entrance should be around here somewhere . . .' said Ember. She unfurled the map again, holding it out with her arms wide.

'Here,' Juniper said, pointing to a wiggly black line that indicated a tunnel. 'The map says it starts at the iron arch, but . . . I don't see an entrance anywhere.'

Hans looked around. 'Let the search begin!' he said.

The three of them started kicking leaves away, searching the ground for any signs of a tunnel. But there was no entrance to be seen.

'It's hopeless,' said Juniper at last. 'I should have chosen a different tunnel.' As she spoke, she leant back against the iron arch, and her elbow caught against one of the metal leaves. An almighty creak sounded around them.

Ember grabbed Juniper by the arm and pulled her close. Hans' eyes widened.

The floor began to shudder and shake, as though an earthquake was starting beneath their feet, and a crack formed underneath the arch. It grew larger and larger, the ground opening up like a mouth.

Not wanting to fall into the chasm, Ember edged backwards, pulling Juniper with her, and Hans followed. After a moment or two, the juddering stopped, leaving a large hole in the ground, complete with a set of steps leading downwards.

'A super-secret entrance!' squealed Hans in an excited whisper. 'Fantabulous! Let's go!' And without giving Ember a moment to think, Hans began to hop down the steps into the darkness. Juniper quickly followed.

Taking a deep breath, Ember hurried after them, trying to push aside her protective nerves and let the excited butterflies through. But a familiar niggling worry remained. Juniper had been begging to go on an adventure for weeks. Ember herself had been missing the magic and wonder of Mount Never since she returned from her own adventure on the mountain to Everspring a month earlier. But watching her sister walk down the steps into the darkness . . .

Juniper will be fine, she told herself sternly. If there was even a sniff of danger as they journeyed to discover what was at the centre of the mountain, they could turn back to safety.

As Ember reached the bottom of the stairs, the entrance closed above her, leaving the three of them in total darkness.

'Wait a second,' she called out. Ember took hold of

the Illumitube around her neck and gave it a shake. It was her latest update on an old invention, the Nothing-Goes-Bump-In-The-Light. Instead of a whole jar of luminescent plants, the Illumitube was a small tube of them that could be worn around your neck like a necklace – perfect for adventuring.

With a quick shake, the Illumitube's glow filled the space around them, and, their path lit, they began to walk again.

The tunnel appeared to have been empty of any human visitors for a long time; it was cold and rocky, with spider webs covering the walls.

'These webs look as though they have been here for years,' said Juniper. 'And they're enormous!'

'What do you think we'll find in the middle of the mountain?' asked Hans.

'Knowing Mount Never, it will be something truly magical,' said Ember, her excitement beginning to return.

After a short while, the tunnel came to a fork. Hans whooped and leapt into the air.

'It's the classic adventurer's conundrum!' he shrieked. 'Which way? One road to certain doom, the other to paradise!'

But Ember smiled and shook her head, showing Hans the map. 'Sorry, Hans, it's not quite as exciting as that. The map shows the two paths end up in the same place. They link up a little further on. The one of the left looks a little shorter though. The one on the right seems to zig-zag a bit . . .'

Hans crossed his arms with a sigh. 'Juniper, which way do you want to go?'

Juniper chewed her lip again and then pointed to the left. 'If that one's shorter, we'll get there faster, right, Ember?'

Ember nodded, and rolled up the map and tucked it into her bag, secretly *very* happy to take the shorter route. She didn't want to take any risks on this trip, not with Juniper here. The sooner they got to the centre, the better.

As the trio walked along the path, Hans chatted about his fierce chess match with himself, but, slowly, a chill crept over Ember. She couldn't help feeling as though something wasn't quite right.

She glanced down at her Illumitube. It was still glowing, but somehow the tunnel felt darker.

They walked on. It had become very quiet. Even Hans stopped talking.

'Ember,' whispered Hans finally. 'Does it feel strange in here to you?'

'No,' said Ember, hoping she sounded certain. The silhouettes of Hans and Juniper were getting harder to see, but the soft blonde colour of her sister's hair still glowed faintly in the dim light. 'It's a bit darker maybe—'

But before she could finish, Hans let out a yelp.

'Hans?' Ember called. She could no longer see his silhouette. She stepped forward – and instead of solid ground, her foot met with nothing but air. Her stomach lurched. Before she could rebalance, Juniper bumped into her from behind, and Ember was launched into space.

With an 'oof' she landed on her back, and found herself slipping and sliding downwards. The tunnel had turned into a steep slide!

Juniper's scream followed a moment later and Ember could hear her sister skidding down the tunnel above her head. Ember flailed her arms out as the three of them slid further and further down into the mountain.

'Wooooo-eeee!' shrieked Hans in front of her.

Ember reached out for something to grab, but the tunnel was smooth and slippery, with no handholds. The three of them hurtled through the underground, unable to see anything in front of them, until finally, the ground levelled out and they slowed, crashing into one another as they came to a stop.

'That was INCREDIBLE!' shouted Hans, always

happy to have an adventure take an unexpected turn.

'I guess the two paths weren't quite the same,' said Juniper, as they got to their feet, pointing. To the left of the slide they'd just emerged from, another path connected to the tunnel; this one contained a set of ordinary, safe-looking steps, leading upwards.

'Never mind,' said Ember, rubbing the dirt off her knees and making a mental note to go back the other way. 'It looks as though we're nearly there.'

Ahead, a light shone at the end of the tunnel, and Ember heard Hans softly squeal under his breath with excitement.

'Wait!' called Juniper. 'Look!'

She pointed at a nearby cobweb that stretched from the wall of the tunnel right across the ceiling above them. There, hanging in the middle, was a fuzzy brown ball.

Ember frowned. 'What is that? Mud from the tunnel?' she asked.

Juniper shook her head. 'That's an egg, I'm sure of it.'

'I thought eggs were hard and made of shell?' said Hans. 'That looks too fluffy to be an egg.'

'We don't know what it is,' said Ember. 'So let's leave it and keep going.'

But Juniper was already reaching up to pull the brown ball free from the web. 'No way. This could be somebody's baby,' she said. 'From everything I know about eggs, they shouldn't be left unguarded. And it's far too cold in here for an egg without its mother. We can't just leave it – it might not survive!'

'Fine,' Ember said, still certain it was nothing more than a ball of tunnel dirt. 'We're close to the centre now, so let's keep going.'

'It looks like a spider's egg, but much bigger,' said Juniper, as she tucked the ball into her jacket to keep it warm. 'Maybe it's a creature I've not read about yet.'

'You know so much about animals,' said Hans in awe. 'I'm happy you're here, Juniper. This is going to be the *best* adventure yet!'

They continued walking and, step by step, closed the distance to the end of the tunnel. There, the narrow passage opened before them into a brightly lit, immense space.

They were clearly in the very centre of Mount Never. As Ember peered up, she realised the whole centre of the mountain was hollow; she could see all the way up to the mountain's peak, which was a blurry point in the distance above her. Below the peak was a shimmering layer, which looked almost liquid. And all around them, spider webs had been woven and sculpted to create incredible structures. Ember could hardly believe her eyes. There were roundhouses made from web, balls made of web, even web hammocks.

But as they stepped over the threshold from tunnel to mountain centre, something twisted in Ember's stomach and a thought rang clear in her mind.

If there were this many spider webs . . . and the hammocks and houses were that large, then that meant . . .

The brown ball Juniper had found *was* an egg.

'E-e-e-ember,' stuttered Hans. 'Are spiders *always* that big?'

An enormous spider, as tall as Juniper, was scuttling towards them, over the webs. Then another appeared. One by one, spiders emerged from their web homes until there were *hundreds* darting towards them.

Hans leapt into Ember's jacket as she pulled Juniper behind her back.

Everywhere she looked, spiders were rushing towards them.

There were more eyes and legs than she could count, and as far as she could tell . . .

They did *not* look happy.

2

Ember inched away from the spiders.

It felt as though her heart had become lodged in her throat.

There was nowhere to hide, and running from hundreds of spiders with legs much longer than her own didn't seem like an option.

So she kept slowly inching back, barely daring to breathe as the spiders came closer and closer until . . .

Suddenly, they stopped.

Ember could hear her and Juniper's hearts drumming out a rhythm in synchronised panic.

The spiders did not move. Was this their chance? Should they run?

The silence was unbearable, like a standoff, each of them waiting to see who moved first.

Then a large web house right in the middle of the mountain rustled. A spider, bigger than all of the others emerged and pushed its way into the crowd, the sea of spiders parting as it moved towards Ember, Juniper and Hans.

All eight of its terrifying eyes glared at Ember. Long legs, hairy and threatening, pulled it forwards, the pincers beneath its face clicking together like jaws.

Ember made up her mind.

'Juniper,' Ember whispered. 'Run.'

Juniper stiffened behind her but didn't move.

The big spider was still edging forward, each step more menacing than the last.

'So,' it snarled, its voice heavy and deep. 'It's *you* who has been trespassing in our thread factory? *You* are the one trying to destroy Mount Never?'

'What?' yelped Ember. 'No! Never, no we—'

Ember couldn't find the right words. She felt Hans sink down inside her jacket, hiding himself completely.

The spider stopped, inches from her face. Ember couldn't see all eight eyes any more; it was so close she could only focus on one.

'We . . . we were just exploring,' she said, balling her hands into fists and trying not to stammer. 'W-we followed a tunnel on a map. We'll go home.'

Her words hung hopefully in the air, until the spider opened its terrifying mouth.

'Get them,' it whispered.

Hundreds of legs leapt into action, spiders hurtling towards them as fast as they could.

'Wait!' shouted Juniper, pushing Ember out of the way. 'Is this yours?' She held the egg up to the largest spider, her arms outstretched.

The largest spider raised a single leg and the others around it stopped in unison. 'Where . . . where did you find that?'

Ember gripped her sister's elbow and tried to pull her back behind her, but Juniper stood firmly in place.

'I spotted it hanging from a web in the tunnel,' Juniper said. She stepped forward ever so slowly and held the egg closer to the enormous spider. 'I thought it looked like an egg, and well, I know how important eggs are . . . and that they should never be left alone.'

Ember held her breath. What was Juniper *doing*? They might think she had *stolen* the egg, and then what would happen?

The spider's eyes narrowed as it stared at Juniper.

After what felt like for ever, the spider broke the silence.

'Thank you,' it said. 'We thought we had lost this one. When they're nearly ready to hatch, they start to move about on their own. It's hard to keep track of them all.'

Juniper smiled kindly. The spider took the egg from Juniper and passed it to another nearby.

'No problem,' Juniper said. 'But you should know, we'd never harm your mountain. This is *Ember Shadows*,' she said importantly.

The spider's eyes flicked to Ember, then back to Juniper. 'So?'

'You know, the girl who *saved* the mountain,' explained Juniper.

'What are you talking about?' the spider said. It twitched its front leg, and the other spiders retreated a short distance from them. Ember felt her shoulders relax the smallest bit.

'You don't know?' whispered Juniper. She stepped forward, and slowly, reached out her hand. 'What's your name? We can tell you everything.'

The spider's eight eyes flitted between them. Finally, it said, 'Lacey.'

'I'm Juniper,' she said with a smile. 'This is Ember, like I said. And that's Hans.'

Hans poked his head out of Ember's jacket, gave a wave, and then nestled down again.

'Tell me what you mean about saving the mountain,' said Lacey, looking concerned.

'It's a little complicated, but I'll try,' Juniper said.

Ember shook her head. Within a split second, they had gone from potential spider food to . . . whatever this was!

'I'll start at the beginning,' said Juniper. She let out a long breath and then began, her voice steady and confident. 'Every human has a Thread of Fate and Mount Never is where all those fates are kept,' she said. 'The threads were meant to be free to roam up and down the mountain through all the different realms: the Know-It-Hall where knowledge is kept, the Forest of Time which determines when a person dies, and the Garden of Gifts, filled with talents and skills. Depending on what their human did down in our village and what decisions they made, the threads should have gained things from those realms, like knowledge, fears, and talents.'

Lacey tapped her leg impatiently. 'What do you mean they were *meant* to be able roam up and down the mountain? Isn't that what they were doing?'

'Someone called Moira was using a machine to trap the Threads of Fate so they couldn't move any more,' Juniper said calmly. 'That meant their human's fate couldn't change. She sent white Fate Cards down to us, telling us what we would become and when we would die. The power of the machine holding our threads, mixed with our belief in the cards, meant our fate simply couldn't be changed. If she wrote on our card we would be a teacher, that's what we'd be. If she said we'd die at eighty-nine, that's when we would die.'

Ember squeezed Juniper's hand. It had only been a few weeks since Ember and Hans had stopped Moira. The thought of those terrible Fate Cards still made her shudder.

'She wrote on my Fate Card that I would die at eight,' said Juniper bravely. 'I'm eight now, so when I got my card, I thought I didn't have much time left. I was scared. Ember went up Mount Never to try and save my life. When she found out that it wasn't the magic of the mountain deciding fates, but a terrible woman named Moira, Ember stopped her and set all the fates free. Now all the threads can move around the magical realms of the mountain again. Our fates can change.'

Lacey took a step backwards. 'Is this true?'

Ember nodded. Neither she, nor anyone else in Everspring, would forget the way each Fate Card had descended from the mountain's peak, landing on its recipient's doorstep. Each card had been packed full of information, telling that person exactly how their life would turn out.

Since Ember had stopped them, the decades of

living bound to a single fate were truly over. Now, everyone was free to choose their own destiny and decide how to live their life.

'So you can see, Ember would never try to destroy the mountain,' said Juniper. 'None of us would.'

'And this woman . . . this *Moira*. Where is she now?' asked Lacey.

The breath caught in the back of Ember's throat. 'She had been cheating death for a hundred years,' she said. 'Hans and I made sure she wouldn't be able to do that any more. She's . . . she's dead.'

Lacey stared intently at Ember and then, seeming to make a decision, she turned and signalled the spiders, who had all been listening without a sound, to leave. As one, like an ocean wave, they scurried back to their web homes.

'It is time for me to tell you something now,' Lacey said, her voice softer. 'You mention the Threads of Fate, but not who creates them. *We* make them. When someone is born, we weave their thread, and it comes out the top of the mountain. It's our duty to protect the threads until the moment they leave the top of our mountain. After that, you humans have free will –

21

protecting your thread is up to you. But we didn't know someone was . . . was . . .'

A tear fell from one of the spider's eyes.

Juniper reached forward and gently stroked a leg. 'You *couldn't* have known,' she said.

Ember swallowed, the last bits of her fear washing away. Juniper had always been good with animals, and it appeared giant, talking spiders were no different.

'And you . . .' said Lacey, pointing a leg at Hans as he emerged from the top of Ember's jacket once more. 'How do you fit into all of this?'

'I'm from the Forest of Time realm,' explained Hans, still looking a little nervous, but gaining confidence as Lacey listened respectfully. 'There, everyone has a tree and a clock showing when they'll die. The Fateweaver – Moira – she snapped me off *her* clock to stop her from aging. Now, I'm a walking talking wonder! *And* I'm Ember's best friend in the whole world.'

'In that case,' said Lacey, 'I think you'd all better come with me.'

She turned and began scuttling through the webs towards the centre of the mountain. They didn't seem to have much choice but to follow. Ember grabbed Juniper's hand firmly and they set off.

As they walked through the web constructions, they passed a group of spiders weaving. Fibres poured out from each front leg, and the spiders wove them together into a single long thread, which Ember recognised as a Thread of Fate.

Near the centre of the mountain, Lacey came to a stop and pointed one leg out to a spot on the floor. Ember, Hans and Juniper huddled around, and Ember's skin prickled as she saw what Lacey was pointing at.

A set of grubby footprints had been left behind on the stone floor.

Someone had been inside the mountain.

'But no one else knows how to get in here!' said Ember, bewildered. 'We have the only map.' Even as she said it, she realised it might not be true. She had the only map she *knew* about but there may have been others.

'Map or no map, someone has been in here, undetected,' said Lacey. 'We found these yesterday evening; it's possible whoever it is has been up on the mountain too. Are you certain Moira is no longer up there?'

'A hundred per cent,' said Ember, as the memory of Moira disintegrating into ash flashed across her mind.

'Could anyone else have been up there since your own journey?'

Ember hadn't considered someone else might want to climb the mountain. The village's Council Leader, Ms Daylands, had only given Ember special permission to explore the mountain's tunnels and its centre today in case there were any other dangers they should be aware of. No one else in Everspring was allowed on the mountain.

Ember shook her head. 'I don't think so . . . but I don't know.' *Had someone else from Everspring wanted to see the Threads of Fate for themselves?* she wondered.

'It is our sworn responsibility to protect the Threads of Fate,' Lacey was saying. 'We can do that inside here, but once they leave the mountain top, we can't protect them. Anyone could take them, or . . .'

She trailed off, the possibilities hanging in the air.

Taking a person's thread meant having a power over them, like holding them hostage. But they could do worse than that. Moira had once threatened to cut

Juniper's thread, which would have killed her instantly.

'We should check the realms for any signs of an intruder,' said Ember, pulling the map from her bag and laying it on the ground. 'Now.'

Juniper and Hans gathered round and Ember began to search for the best route on to the mountain.

'When you stopped Moira,' said Lacey, 'did you ever think about what effect it would have?'

Ember frowned. 'What do you mean?'

'Before you exposed Moira, no one knew that the mountain and its fates could be controlled,' said Lacey. 'Now, they do. Who knows what people will do with that knowledge?'

Ember swallowed. Lacey was right.

Hans touched her hand, bringing her attention back to the map. He pointed to one black line. 'This tunnel looks like it goes from where we are to the Forest of Time,' he said, offering a small smile. 'That's the closest realm.'

With a nod, Ember gathered up the map and slid it back into her backpack.

'I know where that tunnel is,' said Lacey, offering a leg to help Ember up. 'Let me show you.'

Ember smiled and thanked her, but as they followed the giant spider, her thoughts knotted into webs of worry.

Why was someone trespassing inside the mountain? Had they gone to the realms, too? Were they interfering with the Threads of Fate somehow?

Ember wasn't sure she wanted to find out.

3

As they hurried through the tunnel, the three friends barely said a word. Juniper gripped Ember's hand without complaint, and Hans clung to the inside of her jacket.

Ember *knew* she shouldn't have brought Juniper to Mount Never. It was too dangerous. She'd been stupid to think everything was safe just because she'd stopped Moira.

Still, they had no choice now but to continue.

Ahead of them, the tunnel came to a fork. According to the map, the left side stretched out back towards Everspring, while the right would lead them to the Forest of Time. Silently, they hurried along the right-hand path until, after a few minutes, it came to an end in a curtain of leaves. Ember rushed forward to pull the curtain aside. Hans leapt out of her jacket and bounced ahead, into the Forest of Time.

'Hello, old friends!' he yelled cheerily to the trees.

27

The forest was as beautiful as the day Ember had first entered it. They were immediately surrounded by a wave of ticking sounds, which swirled around them. Everywhere Ember turned was a different kind of tree: oak, beech, magnolia . . . each with a clock hanging from its branches. She knew now that each clock belonged to a person beneath, and the time on its face showed when a person was destined to die.

In one important way, however, the forest was very different than the last time she'd been there. Then, the times had been fixed. Now, every single clock was changing time constantly. No one's fate was fixed any more, so the age they would die was completely undetermined.

And there was something else different about the forest this time: the threads that shot around their ankles, hundreds of different colours zooming around them like excited rabbits.

Ember saw Juniper's face, full of wonder, and a burst of happiness flooded through her. She had forgotten how amazing the mountain had seemed to her when she had set foot on it for the first time. Juniper must be feeling that now.

'It's so . . .' Juniper started, but it seemed she couldn't find the words.

'Magical?' asked Ember with a smile.

Juniper nodded, entranced by the ticking forest around them.

Unfortunately, they didn't have time to enjoy it. They were there to find out if someone had been on the mountain.

Ember looked around. 'Now, where should we sta—'

'No, no, no, no!' A cry made them turn. It was Hans.

Ember ran to where Hans knelt, holding two pieces of a single Thread of Fate.

'No,' whispered Ember, staring in horror. Someone had cut the thread.

Around Hans were remnants of other broken threads. An orange one severed in two, a brown one frayed and left just inches from its other half . . .

It was awful.

'Is that . . .' began Juniper, whispering as though she were unable to say the words, looking at what Hans was holding. Her face had turned as pale as the first drops of snow.

Ember nodded, blinking back tears. 'It's a Thread of Fate,' she said. 'Someone *has* been on Mount Never. And they've cut the threads, which means . . .'

'People are dead,' finished Hans, between sobs.

Ember shook her head, as if trying to shake free the horror of what was happening.

How could anyone do this?

'We . . . we have to go,' she stammered, checking the map for the fastest route home. 'Now. We need to show Ms Daylands.'

But Juniper said nothing. Neither did Hans, who sat frozen, his tiny hands full of thread.

'Come on!' Ember shouted, scared by the panic in her own voice.

Neither of them seemed able to move. Ember pushed the map into her bag and carefully collected each of the threads that lay scattered on the floor. There were too many to count. Gingerly, she placed them inside her bag. Then, she lifted Hans into her jacket, took Juniper's hand, and led them back to the tunnel.

The whole time, a single thought throbbed in her mind.

Someone has been cutting threads.

How could someone do such a terrible thing? The thought of it was bad enough, but to *do* it . . .

She wanted to pull Juniper along, to snap her into a run, but her sister was walking slowly, as though she were in a trance, each step an effort.

No one said a word as Ember guided them out of the forest through the curtain of leaves and along the tunnel to the fork they'd passed before. Instead of returning to the mountain's centre, they took the path for Everspring. Finally, they reached a set of stairs leading up to another curtain of leaves and the end of the tunnel.

'Ember, look,' mumbled Hans, pointing to the side of the stairs.

Ember stopped. There was a small wooden door to the left of the stairs, the same shade as Ember's auburn hair.

The door had a simple round brass handle, and above was a small slit in the wood, with a white, rectangular sign that read, *Tickets, please.*

There, next to the sign, was a familiar symbol.

It had been carefully drawn on to the door with silver paint: the outline of four mountain peaks in a circle, surrounded by the letters N, E, S, and W.

Ember knew that symbol. It was on the corner of her map. And Moira had worn a badge with the symbol on her lapel.

Ember pushed her curiosity aside. The symbol was a mystery that had played on her mind ever since the day she had been given the map to Mount Never. But right now, it wasn't important.

'We have to find Ms Daylands,' she said. 'We need to let her know what's happening.'

Hans nodded, and they turned away from the door and instead climbed the set of steps out of the tunnel. They emerged a few metres from the iron arch, near where the first tunnel had begun.

Everspring lay ahead of them, and a terrible thought surfaced for Ember.

Had the threads belonged to anyone she knew?

She knew that Mount Never looked after threads for people who lived both inside and beyond Everspring, though how far beyond her village, she wasn't sure.

'We need to hurry,' said Ember. She pulled Hans from her jacket, placed him on the floor, and began to sprint towards home.

As she did, Juniper seemed to snap back into reality, and together with Hans, the sisters rushed towards the village, heading for the path that led to the Council Hut and Border River.

Ember's vision blurred, tears threatening to stream down her face at any moment. But she couldn't cry. Not yet. She had to fix this.

Finally, she reached the door of the large, round Council Hut building and pounded her fist on the wooden panels.

'Whatever is going on?' came Ms Daylands' voice from inside.

The door opened, but at the sight of Ms Daylands' face, Ember froze. How could she say such a terrible thing aloud?

Juniper skidded to a halt behind her.

'Girls, what's happening?' Ms Daylands asked, her eyes flitting between the two of them. 'I'm in a meeting. Is everything all right?' She was wrapped in a long cloak, which was a rich purple colour, and her tight grey curls bounced in a sort of aura around her head as she looked between Ember and Juniper.

Ember still couldn't find the words. Instead, she

swung her bag round to her front, and pulled out a handful of the threads. Ms Daylands' eyes widened.

'Are they—'

Ember nodded.

'You'd better come inside,' Ms Daylands said. She glanced around, then beckoned them in, and closed the door behind them.

In the circular hall, sitting in front of Ms Daylands' desk at the back of the room, were two people Ember didn't recognise.

The first, a man with golden hair and dark brown eyes, smiled brightly at Ember as she entered, but when he spotted the threads in her hands and the expression on her face, his smile disappeared. He stood, stumbling slightly, and metallic bangles chimed on his wrists, clattering as he pulled another three chairs up to Ms Daylands' desk.

'Sit, sit!' he said. 'This is clearly urgent.' He hovered for a moment, as if not sure whether to stay or go. 'Look, Wisteria, why don't I come back—'

'Stay, if you don't mind, Haywood,' interrupted Ms Daylands. 'We may need your assistance.'

The man nodded and returned to sit beside the

other person in the room, a boy who looked around Ember's age. He hadn't moved since the trio had entered but was staring at the threads intently. His dark hair flopped over brown eyes framed with a set of particularly long eyelashes.

Ember, Juniper and Hans sat down in silence. Ember clutched the threads tighter, though she didn't know why she wanted to hold on to them. She felt Juniper move closer, until her hand was tucked in the crook of Ember's elbow.

'Ember, Juniper, Hans,' said Ms Daylands slowly. 'This is Haywood Larkin. He was a Council Leader in Overwood, another village not far from here, until recently . . .'

She trailed off and coughed awkwardly, but Haywood simply held out a hand in greeting.

'He's . . . been relieved of his duties,' said Ms Daylands, composing herself, 'and has *kindly* come to Everspring to see if he could help us as we adjust to living without Fate Cards.'

'Ember Shadows,' he said. 'I've certainly heard a lot about you.' He wore long chains around his neck, strung with bright gemstone beads which shone in the candlelight. Around his waist, he had a loop of rope hanging from his belt, and a knife in a leather pouch with a dark brown handle.

Ms Daylands began again, gesturing at the boy. 'And this is his—'

'Apprentice,' said Haywood. 'Falcon.'

The boy looked up to Ember and nodded.

No one said anything for a long moment. Everyone's eyes were fixed on Ember.

'Ember?' Ms Daylands prompted. 'Do you want to explain what's happened?'

With a deep breath, Ember carefully laid the threads on the desk. They seemed so ordinary, like any normal threads. She focused on one, silver and almost as thick as her little finger, but lifeless and broken in two.

Those on the mountain were so full of life, so animated – she had never imagined seeing a thread like this . . .

'We found these in the Forest of Time,' Ember said. 'They've been cut.'

There was another long silence. Eventually, Hans broke it.

'Whoever these threads belonged to,' Hans

whispered, 'are they really . . . dead?'

Ms Daylands clasped her hands together and nodded softly. 'I'm afraid so.' She picked up a glass jar, gathered the threads up gently, and placed them inside. 'Let's keep them safe, shall we? Tell me, Ember – why were you in the Forest of Time in the first place? I thought you were journeying to the centre of Mount Never.'

Ember explained that they had chosen a tunnel and visited the centre of Mount Never. She told her about the spiders who spun the Threads of Fate, and the strange set of footprints.

'So, we went up to the realms to check they were safe,' finished Ember.

'And you found these?' asked Haywood, grimacing.

Juniper and Ember nodded in unison.

'Were there any others?' Ms Daylands asked.

Tears began to escape from Ember's eyes as she tried to blink them back. 'I don't know,' she said. 'We saw these and—'

'What are we going to do?' said Juniper, her voice small but determined. It was the first time she had spoken since they had found the threads.

Ms Daylands took in a deep breath and ran her

hand over the outside of the jar.

'Maybe it was just their time?' suggested Haywood hopefully. 'People's Threads of Fate must break at some point, when they get old . . .'

'Look at how the ends of the threads are frayed,' Ms Daylands said, pointing. 'Someone struggled to cut these threads. No. There was nothing natural about these deaths.'

Ember felt a shiver go down her spine.

'I wonder if this is happening at any of the other mountains,' said Ms Daylands with a frown.

'There are more?' asked Hans in surprise.

'That's what the myths say,' Ms Daylands said thoughtfully. 'More mountains, and more magical landscapes. Places that control fate, our emotions, the natural world. A rather eccentric author called Hans Christof Sanderson wrote a whole collection of stories about them. My goodness, I think there's even a legend about a landscape that controls time itself!'

Something lit up in Ember's mind like the spark of an idea, but as she glimpsed the jar full of threads, their lifeless shapes piled at the bottom, it flickered and extinguished.

'Anyway, that's not our priority right now,' said Ms Daylands. 'Haywood, I think we need to call an emergency village meeting for first thing tomorrow morning.'

'Absolutely,' he said. 'It would be a pleasure to help in any way possible; that's why I'm here.'

'Ms Daylands,' asked Ember, finally voicing her biggest worry, 'do we know who has died?'

'No one has come to me with such terrible news,' said Ms Daylands. 'We'll do a village-wide check, of course, but Mount Never is responsible for more than just Everspring's fates, my dear. These deaths may have happened miles away from here. We'll need to alert people far and wide.'

'How?'

'I'll contact village representatives by radio right away. We will ask one from each village under Mount Never's influence to come to tomorrow's meeting. Haywood, will you send for your village's new leaders?'

'No need,' he said. 'I can send news back to Overwood myself after the meeting tomorrow.'

Ms Daylands nodded, then turned back to Ember, Juniper and Hans. 'Go home and try to get some sleep,'

40

she said. 'We'll need you here bright and early for the meeting tomorrow.'

Ember and Juniper looked at one another, and Hans climbed into Ember's jacket.

'It's been a pleasure,' said Haywood, holding out his hand to Ember, 'in spite of the circumstances. It's good to put a face to the person behind the end of the Fate Cards.'

Ember smiled politely and they left the hut, slowly walking back to their home in silence.

Only when they were a few strides from the front door of their roundhouse did Hans finally speak.

'Are you OK?' he asked Ember, much more quietly than usual.

'It's just . . . not fair,' said Ember. 'I was trying to *fix* things, not make them worse. Once I saved Juniper and set everyone's fate free, I really thought things would be better.'

Hans nodded. 'But now . . .'

'But now *this*,' she agreed. 'And it's all my fault,' she went on. 'Without me, no one would have ever known about the threads or the possibility that they could be cut.'

Juniper squeezed Ember's hand. 'I'm still glad you did what you did. You set everyone free. And you saved my life after all.'

Ember tried to smile. She *had* saved Juniper and she didn't regret that for a second. But the image of those broken threads wouldn't shift from her mind.

It felt as though she had pushed one domino over, and a whole line of them was now slowly crashing down.

She only hoped she could find a way to stop them.

4

Standing outside the Council Hut the next morning, Ember put on a brave face and smiled to Juniper.

'It's going to be OK,' she said.

Juniper twisted her hair in her fingers but said nothing.

Exchanging a worried look with Hans, who was tucked into her jacket, Ember stepped inside.

Her mother had arrived early to help set up, foreseeing a large turnout – and she had been right. The Council Hut was packed. Rows and rows of chairs had been squeezed into the circular space. Those who couldn't find a seat were standing around the edges, while children sat on the floor. Ember scanned the crowd and realised for the first time in her life, there were more people there that she *didn't* recognise than those she did. As Ms Daylands had planned, representatives from nearby villages had travelled overnight to join the emergency meeting, all anxious to hear the news.

As she pushed through to reach her mum, who was keeping a seat for them at the front, the crowd fell silent.

Everyone's eyes were on her.

No one knew why they were here . . . but they all knew what she had done.

Before Ember had travelled up the mountain, their lives had been simple, all laid out for them on a Fate Card. But now, everyone had to make decisions for themselves. A lot of people were enjoying that freedom, but Ember knew others felt as though their lives had been thrown into chaos, and some of them blamed her for it.

Ember sank into a chair next to her mum.

'It's going to be OK,' her mum said, reaching out for Ember's hand and offering a warm smile to Hans. But despite having told Juniper the exact same thing, Ember wasn't so sure.

As Juniper sat down on Ember's other side, the clip-clop of Ms Daylands' heels announced her arrival. Today's cloak, a ruby red colour with grey fur trim, swished at her feet as she headed towards the front. Haywood followed, dressed as he was the day before.

Ember scanned the room for Falcon and caught a glimpse of his hair at the back of the hall. He met her gaze, then quickly looked away.

Ms Daylands reached the front, then cleared her throat as she faced the crowd. 'Right,' she said, briskly. 'Thank you all for coming. First, let me introduce you to Haywood Larkin. He was Council Leader of Overwood before the Fate Cards were changed. He has come to see if his talents can be used here.'

Haywood stepped forward. 'Thrilled to be here,' he said. 'Like Everspring, my village was under Moira's control. When the cards changed there was a terrible, dangerous uprising. Many people wanted to be Council Leader. I negotiated the conflicts and peacefully paved the way for a new leader to take the reins. Then, I embraced the opportunity to find more villages I could help and came to Everspring. And with the challenge we face today, I'm very pleased I did.'

Ms Daylands nodded in thanks. 'Haywood's help comes not a moment too soon, as we have an emergency on our hands.'

A murmur crept through the crowd.

'I regret to tell you,' began Ms Daylands, 'that

45

someone has chosen a destiny darker than any I could have imagined. Someone has climbed Mount Never to hunt Threads of Fate.' She paused, taking a deep breath before continuing. 'They have cut these threads, *killing* the people they belong to.'

Gasps filled the room, then whispers, shocked voices gathering momentum until they died down like a wave as Ms Daylands raised her hands.

'Now, my question is simple,' she said. 'Does anyone have information about this criminal?' Her voice was burning with anger.

No one said a word.

Ms Daylands let the silence creep around the room, filling every corner.

'No one?' she said.

Finally, a hand shot up. 'Have you asked *her*?'

Ember's skin prickled. She knew they were talking about her without even turning around.

'Ember is the one who *found* the cut threads,' said Ms Daylands with an impatient sigh.

'Convenient!' called another voice.

Hands began to shoot up around the hall. Ember sank further into her chair.

'She made this mess,' shouted a man from the back. 'All of it – threads, Fate Cards, it's her fault. I used to know what I was doing with my life. Now I can't even decide which socks to put on in the morning.'

Other voices yelled out in agreement.

Ms Daylands clapped her hands together. 'You are missing the point!' she shouted. Ember jolted. She had never known Ms Daylands shout. 'Someone is *cutting threads*, killing people from afar, seemingly totally at random. Do you understand the severity of the situation? Now is not the time to turn on each other. We must come together to stop this thing.'

The hall was silent.

Finally, a woman spoke up. '*How* do we stop it?'

Ms Daylands rubbed her temples. 'Gather as much information as you can from your villages,' she said. 'We need help in identifying who the victims of the cut threads were. If you know of anyone who has passed away suddenly, please speak to us.'

'And remember to report anything you think might be suspicious,' urged Haywood.

On the front row along from Ember, Mr Coal, her schoolteacher, raised his hand. 'Does this mean *anyone* could have their thread cut at any time?' he asked.

Ms Daylands nodded sympathetically. 'I'm afraid so.'

'In the circumstances,' said Haywood, 'my advice is to live each day as if it is your last.'

'But how do we know the *right* way to live each day?' called a woman from behind Ember.

'That's the struggle isn't it?' said Haywood. 'I, too, am finding it a challenge. We were each given a purpose on our card, and it has been snatched away from us, stolen in the night.' He looked at Ember, his eyes kind. 'Ember never intended anything like this, I'm sure. But nevertheless we must all live with the consequences.'

Ember felt her cheeks redden.

'The Fate Card simply showed one possible purpose and path for your life,' said Ms Daylands. 'You can still follow what was written on your card if you like. But it's *your* decision now. You can *choose*.'

'I can't make a decision,' said Mr Coal, his voice cracking. 'Every time I think I've decided, I wonder if it's the right thing to do.'

'It's certainly a challenge,' said Haywood. 'Sometimes I wonder if the Fate Cards were easier, but—'

'The challenge is part of life's beauty,' Ms Daylands finished with a smile. 'It takes great courage to do what you believe to be right without knowing for sure.'

'I preferred things the way they were before,' called a man, and there was a chorus of agreement.

Ms Daylands raised her hand and soon, the room fell quiet. 'Look, Ember was faced with an impossible decision,' she said. 'Allow her sister to die or free us from the Fate Cards and the control of Moira's machine. None of us can say we would have chosen differently.' She paused and let out a long breath. 'Now, if no one has any information about who is cutting the threads, we will end this meeting.'

Slowly, the hall emptied.

Ember, her mum, Juniper and Hans sat in silence, waiting for the last people to leave. All the while, Ember was consumed with one thought.

Ms Daylands had made it sound as though there had been only two options, but really, Ember knew otherwise. There had been a third option.

She could have saved Juniper and left the fates under the machine's control.

Moira had created a machine that did all the work for her. Ember could have easily changed Juniper's fate and then adapted Moira's machine so it would carry on sending Fate Cards out for ever. Then, everyone would have been able to live happily under the comfort of a pre-written fate.

No one would have known the mountain could be controlled. No one would have known they could cut threads.

It *was* her fault.

Ember peeled her hand from her mum's, pulled Hans from her jacket and placed him on the ground, and stood up.

'I'm going home,' she said.

'But Ember—' started Hans.

Ember shook her head and left the Council Hut alone. As she walked back home, her thoughts knotted together, one weaving its way into the next.

Maybe it was better when everyone had a pre-determined fate, Ember thought. *Maybe the mountain would have been safer if I had stopped Moira, but not exposed her.*

She looked up at Mount Never. The long wooden house that teetered on its peak was seesawing wildly back and forth. Moira had told her that the house would only balance when the world beneath was running in harmony, like it had when everyone had a set fate to follow.

Since Ember had destroyed the machine, it had been swinging more wildly each day.

How would she ever be able to trust herself to make the right decision again?

'Ember!' shouted a familiar voice, snapping her from her trance. She turned to find Ms Daylands hurrying up the path behind her. 'The map to Mount Never and its realms,' she said breathlessly. 'You're keeping it safe, yes?

'Yes,' said Ember, who kept the map with her always. 'But what are we going to do?'

'Nothing,' Ms Daylands said. 'Not yet anyway.'

'But more people could be hurt at any moment! Who knows how many threads that person could—'

'Ember, whoever is doing this clearly has nothing to lose,' interrupted Ms Daylands sternly. 'They have a plan, an evil one. We can't possibly go up against some mysterious figure without a plan of our own.'

Ember bit her lip. If she had followed Ms Daylands' advice last time, Juniper might be dead by now.

'But—'

'Please,' said Ms Daylands. 'Do not go looking for this person. Let Haywood and I handle this one.'

Ember seethed with frustration and looked at the floor. How could she sit back when people were dying?

Ms Daylands took a step forward and reached out, placing her hand on Ember's shoulder. 'Are you OK, my dear?'

'Not really,' Ember said with a sniff. 'I thought stopping Moira was the right thing to do. For the first few weeks people seemed happy, but now . . .'

Ms Daylands sighed. 'Freedom is difficult. For some

people, it's overwhelming.'

Ember knew that. Her own Fate Card had arrived blank – the first ever to arrive without a destiny. Back then, she had been terrified.

Then she had an idea. 'Moira told me that there was a lot of the world still left for her to control,' Ember said. 'Maybe we need to find someone who never got a card. They can help us figure out what is right and wrong.'

'I had the same idea,' said Ms Daylands. 'A few weeks ago, I reached out to a village far away from all of this mess to see if someone from there might visit us.'

She stepped back and raised her eyebrows. 'But you need to start believing in yourself a bit more, Ember. I have no doubt that you will *always* do what is right. Don't forget what you did for Flint. He's thriving thanks to you.'

It was true. Flint had lived on Mount Never without a Fate Card for years, so he knew how to make decisions. Since Ember had reunited him with his parents, he had been working as an inter-village post officer. He seemed to be the only person in Everspring who had decided on his purpose and confidently stuck with it, exploring other villages and carrying news and messages between them on his quad-sled. Ember was happy for him, but she missed her friend now he was away so often.

'If you think I'll do the right thing, then why can't I go and look for the person cutting thr—' Ember started.

'No,' said Ms Daylands firmly. 'Saving the world doesn't always mean charging off on an adventure. Sometimes it means planning the next step.'

Ember bristled. They didn't have time for *planning*.

'I won't be here tomorrow, Ember,' continued Ms Daylands. 'I'm trusting you not to go off hunting for the culprit while I'm away.'

'Where are you going?' asked Ember curiously.

'Ah . . . something I need to do,' Ms Daylands said, her eyes darting away from Ember and back quickly. 'Anyway, I must go.' And without another word, she turned, her cloak whipping around her, and left Ember on the path.

Ember looked up at the mountain with a sigh.

She was fed up with people trying to control Mount

Never. And she was fed up with secrets.

Although, she thought as she hurried home, *there is* one *secret that might be useful.*

Once she arrived home, she went straight to her bedroom, pulled the map from her bag, and unfurled it.

There, in the bottom corner, was the strange emblem of four mountain peaks and the letters *N*, *E*, *S*, and *W*. Beneath it was the word S.E.C.R.E.T. It had puzzled her ever since she had been given the map and for a long time she'd had no idea as to what it meant.

But now she had a clue.

The door that Hans had pointed to in the tunnel. It'd had that same symbol on it.

That door . . . it was hidden inside the mountain's tunnels. A person could come and go through it as they pleased without being seen. What if the person cutting threads was coming through it? And if they were somehow connected to this symbol, were they also connected to Moira? After all, she had worn a badge with the symbol on too. Maybe they were coming to finish Moira's work?

Ember took a deep breath, her mind racing. If they were as dangerous as Moira, she had no time to lose. She had to stop this, once and for all.

5

'Don't you think we should tell Juniper?' asked Hans as he bounced on Ember's bed.

As soon as Hans had returned from the Council Hut, he'd come to Ember's bedroom, where he'd found her packing. She'd told him she thought they should try and find out more about the strange symbol and that the door with it on might be a clue. Now she was desperate to get going.

'No way,' Ember said. 'It's far too dangerous for Juniper to come. We almost lost her once, I'm not going to risk it again.'

Hans raised his little eyebrows and looked as though he wanted to say something else, but Ember turned away from him to continue packing and he said nothing.

'I think there's a good chance that whoever cut the Threads of Fate used the strange door we saw in the tunnel,' Ember said to fill the silence. 'It's close to both the centre of the mountain where the footprint was *and* the Forest of Time where the threads were cut.' She turned to the bed where the map was laid out next to Hans and tapped the wax seal in the corner. 'So we should start by getting through that door. It might lead us to them. It's our best bet.'

'That's just because we don't have any other leads,' said Hans glumly.

Ember chose to ignore this. 'There was a sign on the door, wasn't there? *Tickets please.* So we can't get through the door without tickets. Maybe Moira had them. Where did she spend most of her time?'

'Hmmm,' said Hans, scratching his head. 'Either the Messy Middle, or the house on the top of Mount Never.'

Ember thought of the house swinging wildly at the peak of the mountain and her stomach swooped uncomfortably. 'Let's start at the Messy Middle,' she suggested.

She returned to her rucksack and packed a selection of nuts, bolts and scraps of metal along with her favourite silver toolbox that her father had given her. She paused for a moment, brushing her fingers against the cold metal.

Ember missed him every day. He had died saving her from drowning when she was little, and their family had long believed that it had been his fate. But when Ember climbed Mount Never, she discovered that he had been destined to live, only he loved her so much that he managed to break free of Moira's control, save Ember's life, and rewrite both of their destinies.

Now, Ember was determined to make him proud every day. Today, that meant stopping whoever was cutting these threads.

When she was done packing, she turned to Hans, who was studying the map laid on the bed.

'Are you all packed?'

Ember nodded.

'Well then, what are we waiting for?' Hans said. 'Let's go!'

'I have something for you first,' Ember said. 'I was going to give it to you tomorrow, but now seems like a good time.'

Ember pulled open her desk drawer and took out a small dark green box. 'I made this when you said green was your favourite colour, but that was last week and now—'

'It's green again!' said Hans, his eyes wide. He was almost shaking with excitement, his tiny feet tapping the top of the bed. 'I've never had a present before!'

'I hope you like it,' Ember said, and handed him the box.

Before it was fully out of her hands, Hans had ripped the silver ribbon off the top and pulled the lid open. He gasped, his eyes fixed on the invention inside.

'My own Shh!-Oos?!' he whispered. 'You made me *Shh!-Oos!*' Suddenly, he whistled like a firework, sailing through the light bulbs overhead.

'Hans! Calm down.' Ember laughed.

Hans landed on the edge of the bed, his legs swinging over the side, and begged, 'Put them on me! PUT THEM ON!!!'

Ember obliged and, soon enough, Hans was walking, hopping and bouncing around the bedroom, in complete silence – not that his feet had really made that much noise before anyway. It was his voice that was the problem!

'Look at me! Now I'm a goody-two-shoes!' he shouted.

'Hans, *you* still have to be quiet, otherwise there's

not much point having silent shoes.'

Hans pretended to zip his lips and started tiptoeing around the room. Finally, though, words ripped from his mouth. 'I'M SO QUIET!'

'Are you ready?' Ember asked, giggling.

Hans saluted her and mouthed the word *yes*.

Then, wearing their matching Shh!-Oos, they crept silently out of the house.

'Which way then, Navigator?' Hans asked as they stood outside, around the corner from the house so there was no risk of Juniper stepping outside and seeing them.

Ember opened the map, pointing at a tunnel that began not far from the base of the mountain. 'This tunnel should take us straight to the Messy Middle.'

*

Just as the map had promised, the tunnel led Ember and Hans directly to the Messy Middle.

It was an enormous realm, filled with giant snow globes which showed a person's future. Of course, when Moira had the fates in her control, there was only one way each person's life would pan out and the globes were stuck showing only one image for each person. But now, threads ran riot through the realm, scurrying all over the snow globes. Each time a thread touched the glass outside, the life-sized models within would change to a freeze frame of that person's current future, but then might quickly flicker and change into a different future entirely. Then another thread would touch the glass, and the models would change again, showing another person's potential future.

Ember watched as a dark red thread leapt on to the snow globe closest to them.

'Hans, look,' she said, pointing to the freeze frame that had formed inside. 'It's Ms Daylands!'

The snow globe showed Ms Daylands holding something. It looked like a piece of machinery. Her brow was furrowed and she seemed confused.

Before Ember could get a better look, the long

thread leapt from the snow globe and snaked along the floor. Another jumped on to the glass and the freeze frame of Ms Daylands was replaced with an image of a young girl retrieving a very burnt cake from the oven.

'If we had the broken threads with us, we could hold them up to a globe,' said Hans as they stepped forwards, past the snow globe. 'The glass could show us who they belonged to.'

'You're right,' Ember said. Ms Daylands would never have given them the jar though – she didn't even know they were here.

Ember looked out into the dark realm, considering where to search first. Cutting a path through the snow globes was a train track. Last time, Moira's train had taken them on a roller coaster ride that had left Ember shaken and her insides all jumbled up. This time the track looked as though it was staying put on the ground, for the moment at least. Beyond the train track, snow globes, and the mountain's earth beneath their feet, there was little else in the vast realm. It had unnerved Ember last time she had visited, and the feeling began to return now.

Suddenly, a dark brown shape appeared overhead, swooping towards them.

'Florence!' shouted Hans, leaping up with excitement.

The owl came to land in front of them and gave a quick shake of her feathers. Ember's heart filled with relief at the sight of a friendly face. Florence had helped them stop Moira; maybe she could help them again.

'Hello, you two,' she squawked. 'Nice to see you back. Have you heard? There's someone on the mountain again, they're—'

'Cutting threads,' finished Ember. 'We know.'

'Terrible, terrible news!' said Florence. 'It's going to be in tomorrow's paper. The whole mountain is talking about the terrifying Thread-Cutter!'

Florence had started the *Mount Never News* after helping Ember and Hans stop Moira. She probably knew more about the mountain than anyone.

'Has anyone on the mountain seen anything?' Ember asked.

Florence shook her head. 'I'm afraid not. All we know is that the crime must be recent. Only the night before last, I was making my midnight newspaper delivery in the Forest of Time, and there were no cut threads or strange people lurking around then. I assume you two are on the case?' She peered over her glasses.

'Absolutely!' said Hans. 'We're here to look for tickets.'

'Well, no better place than a train for that,' Florence said.

'Exactly,' Ember said, confidence brewing.

'Let's get going then,' said Florence as she took off and together, the three of them followed the winding track.

Either side of them, the snow globes continued to light up, illuminating the realm with flashes of light, flickering on and off each time the models transformed inside. If Ember hadn't been so worried, she would have liked to stop and watch them. It was beautiful how they changed from scene to scene as people determined their own futures.

'Look!' shouted Hans, waddling forwards as fast as he could. 'The train's arrived.'

Ember pulled her gaze away from the globes and ran after him towards the blue-and-white striped train. Its engine carriage puffed out grey steam while its open-topped carriages waited patiently behind, each one big enough for two people. It had come to rest at the end of the track, beside the door to the next realm, the Garden of Gifts.

As she drew closer to the train, a terrible thought crossed Ember's mind.

Was it possible that Moira wasn't dead after all? Would she find her here, slumped in the train like the day they had met?

But thankfully the train was empty, and it appeared to have arrived at the end of the track by itself. On the dashboard in the engine cart, all the different buttons flashed away as if waiting to be used again.

'OK,' Ember said. 'Let's look for the tickets. You two start at the back carriage of the train. I'll start at the front.'

Hans saluted her and Florence took off. Ember sat in the front of the engine carriage and peered under the dashboard. There was nothing there.

She ran her hand over the flashing buttons. *Moira certainly was a good inventor*, she thought. *But this Thread-Cutter seems to be doing even more damage with just a pair of scissors . . .*

She searched the carriage carefully, but there was nothing.

'These seats are like suitcases!' yelled Hans from the back. 'Moira has so many screwdrivers and buttons and bolts and . . .'

Ember frowned. The seats were like suitcases – what did Hans mean? She grabbed the edge of the driver's seat and pulled, to find that it hinged up like a lid.

Her breath beginning to quicken, Ember opened it fully to reveal an entire storage space within. Moira's old clothes were there – a spare blue-and-white suit, conductor's hat, and a bundle of notebooks and pens. Ember opened one of the notebooks and discovered it was full of drawings and designs for the train.

Her heart twisted with a glimmer of sympathy. Moira must have been so lonely.

She reached inside and carefully began to move things. Beneath the books was a small rectangular silver tin that was tarnished in the corners.

'Only inventing stuff in the other carriages,' said Hans from behind her. 'Tools, scraps of metal, blueprints for inventions . . .'

'But no tickets,' finished Florence, landing on the window ledge of the engine carriage.

'What's that?' said Hans, spotting the tin in Ember's hands.

'I'm not sure,' said Ember.

Before she could do anything else, Florence let out a loud squawk. 'Spy! Spy!' she screamed.

Ember and Hans tumbled out of the carriage, Ember's heart hammering against her ribs as she scrambled to her feet.

Could it be the Thread-Cutter?

A panicked voice shouted above Florence's screech. 'No, wait, I'm not a spy!'

'Come out then and show yourself,' called Ember.

Slowly, a figure emerged from behind a snow globe. It was Falcon, the boy Haywood had brought with him to Everspring.

Hans put up his hands like a boxer as Ember stepped back.

'I'm not a spy,' Falcon said again. Ember eyed him suspiciously. He was dressed in dark clothes and a black jacket. Emerging from the shadows, he certainly *looked* like someone who didn't want to be seen. 'I *was* following you, but I—'

'Why?' said Hans, bouncing from one foot to the other. 'Why were you following us?'

Falcon pushed his hair back off his face, then began to twist his hands together.

Ember glared at him. 'Explain,' she said. 'Quickly.'

'We found out who the people were whose threads were cut,' Falcon said. 'The news just came in over the radio. They were people from Overwood.'

Ember's stomach sank. 'That's terrible,' she whispered.

'That doesn't explain why you followed Ember and Hans, whoever you are,' said Florence from her perch on the train roof.

'My name is Falcon,' he said, then he turned back to Ember. 'I could tell that Haywood and Ms Daylands didn't have a plan. Then I saw you heading out of town. You looked like you *did* have a plan, and I wanted to help so . . .'

Ember's shoulders softened. He looked terrified.

'Please,' he said. 'I can't sit around and do nothing.'

Ember remembered the feeling when she had seen Juniper's Fate Card, confirming her imminent death.

Falcon's face was etched with the same helplessness and panic.

'Don't worry,' Ember said. 'Maybe you can help.'

Hans lowered his fists and Florence nodded.

As Hans explained to Falcon that they were looking for tickets to get them through the S.E.C.R.E.T. door where they might find the Thread-Cutter, Ember returned to the tarnished box.

Gently, she pulled off the lid. Inside was a large piece of paper that had been folded twice into a square. Anticipation building, she lifted it out.

It was a letter. At the top, Ember immediately recognised the S.E.C.R.E.T. symbol. She gripped the paper and began to read.

Moira,

As a S.E.C.R.E.T. agent, we believed we could trust you. We are saddened to learn that your reports stating that Mount Never was safe were lies. We know that you have gone against S.E.C.R.E.T. policy, and for over a year now have been fixing fates in place, taking away the

71

free will of others.

This is unacceptable.

You have left us in an impossible situation.

If we leave you to continue your work, you control the lives of thousands.

If we expose you, people will realise the mountains can be controlled. That threads can be manipulated, cut even. The risk of what another person might do with this power is too great.

As an organisation, we have decided the least damaging option is to leave you. We appeal instead to your good nature. We plead that if you continue down this path, you assign fates fairly and with compassion.

We will be watching. Should you do anything we believe outweighs the risk of exposing the mountain, we will remove you.

From this moment forwards, you have been struck off the S.E.C.R.E.T. list. You are no longer part of the organisation and have no right to wear your badge. Destroy any remaining tickets you have, and never contact us again.

Burn after reading.

From,

The Safeguarding Establishment for Curious,
Rare and Enchanted Terrain (S.E.C.R.E.T.)

Ember thought her mind might explode with so much new information.

'Burn after reading?' asked Hans. 'Do we need to make a fire?'

'Don't worry about *that*,' Ember said. 'Don't you understand?'

Hans' face looked blanker than ever. 'Erm . . . Moira had a pen pal?'

'No, silly,' said Ember. 'Moira was a part of this organisation, S.E.C.R.E.T. From the sounds of it, she was meant to *protect* the mountain, not control it.'

'Well, she didn't do a very good job did she?' said Hans.

'No. So S.E.C.R.E.T. fired her,' Ember explained.

'Why didn't they come and stop her instead?' asked Falcon.

Ember bit her lip. 'Because they thought what she was doing was bad, but it wasn't as bad as everyone finding out the mountain could be controlled.'

Hans' eyes widened. 'Which is what happened because of us . . .'

Ember nodded miserably. 'There is *some* good news,' said Hans.

'There is?'

'Terrain means lands, doesn't it?' he said. 'It says they protect *enchanted terrain*! That can't *only* be Mount Never, or they'd be the Mount Never protection team. So does that mean Ms Daylands was right . . . there are more magical landscapes?'

Ember's mind fizzed with the possibility, and she grinned at Hans.

'I think so,' she said. 'And there's another bit of good news too. If S.E.C.R.E.T. didn't like what Moira was doing, they probably aren't the people cutting threads. They might want to help us, and they're probably behind that S.E.C.R.E.T. door. It's got their logo on it, after all.'

Hans leapt into the air and let out a squeal of excitement and Falcon ducked to avoid his path.

'But,' said Ember, focusing her thoughts, 'we still can't get *through* the door. This letter mentions tickets, but it tells Moira to destroy them. Unless . . .'

She peered into the tin again. There was something else inside. It was a stack of small rectangle white cards.

They had the familiar symbol on them, as well as the words:

S.E.C.R.E.T.
One-way admittance to this line only.
Line 431

'Tickets!' said Ember, her heart soaring. Moira hadn't destroyed them as she was meant to.

Hans punched his fists into the air, and whooped in her ear.

'The plan is back in action!' he cried.

'So what exactly *is* the plan?' mumbled Falcon.

'Go through the door, find S.E.C.R.E.T. and ask for help to stop the Thread-Cutter,' said Ember triumphantly.

'Is that *definitely* what you're calling the cutting

person?' Hans asked Florence. 'Surely we can come up with a better name!'

Ember smiled, and gathered Moira's bits together, carefully putting the tin and the letter in her bag, and the tickets in her pocket.

'How about the Frayer?' suggested Hans before Florence could respond. 'The Thread Monster. The Snip-Snap Snooper—'

'Hans,' said Florence sternly. 'Whoever did this is *killing* people. I don't think we should give them a funny name.'

Hans blushed a silvery pink.

Florence looked over her glasses with a hint of mischief. 'Besides, Thread-Cutter is *definitely* what we're calling them. It's in tomorrow's paper, and that's already gone to print.'

Hans grinned back at her. 'Thread-Cutter it is.'

'Now let's go and find out where that door leads,' said Ember.

'Maybe we should go back and tell Haywood and Ms Daylands what we found first,' said Falcon with a sudden boldness. 'They could help us.'

'No way,' said Ember. 'They'd try and stop us.'

'Fine,' Falcon said. 'But I'm coming with you then. I can't sit in the village and do nothing.'

Ember nodded gently. She understood that feeling.

As they set off for the S.E.C.R.E.T. door together, Ember felt a flicker of hope grow inside of her. They might not have found who was behind the thread-cutting yet, but they *had* found tickets. They had discovered what S.E.C.R.E.T. meant. Hopefully the agency would be able to help them.

And no matter what Ms Daylands said, it was better to be looking for answers. After all, Ember knew there was no way of telling when the next thread might be cut.

Or, she thought with a shudder, *whose it could be*.

6

After exiting the tunnel from the Messy Middle at the base of the mountain, the group hurried towards the iron arch. They now needed the tunnel which would take them to the S.E.C.R.E.T. door. It seemed the mountain base was dotted with secret entrances. Without the map, they would no doubt get lost in the criss-crossing maze.

It felt so long ago that they had emerged from this tunnel with Juniper, clutching the broken Threads of Fate, but it had only been yesterday. For a moment, Ember thought of her sister, waiting at home, and wondered whether she was doing the right thing by excluding Juniper from all of this. A seed of guilt planted in her stomach.

'I'll wait here,' said Florence, when they reached the arch and opened the tunnel's entrance. 'If you don't return before sunset, I'll send help.'

Ember bit her lip, the worry over Juniper

disappearing. This could be dangerous, and there was no way she wanted her sister involved in anything dangerous.

'Are you sure about this?' asked Falcon. 'Shouldn't we tell *someone*? Maybe Haywood—'

'I already told you, there's no time to argue with the adults about it,' said Ember. 'We have to go, now.'

She didn't want to say her other reason aloud: that if Juniper found out what was happening, she'd find a way to get involved. She paused, looking at Hans and Falcon. 'Ready?' she asked.

They both nodded (Falcon slightly reluctantly), and together pulled the curtain of leaves aside and began to climb down the steps. Ember glanced back over her shoulder as the leaves fell back, Florence disappearing behind them.

At the bottom of the stairs they found the door with the S.E.C.R.E.T. symbol. Beneath the symbol was the little slot for tickets.

Ember handed each of them a ticket.

'Me first,' Hans said, and before Ember could argue, he was holding out his ticket to the door. The ticket was swiftly sucked into the slot. The door let out a clattering sound and then swung open to reveal a dimly lit tunnel. Hans stepped over the threshold, and the door slammed closed behind him with a loud *clunk*.

Ember lined up her own ticket, the door swung open again, and she stepped through. Falcon followed behind her.

After their adventure on Mount Never, Ember was used to doors opening into strange realms with wild magic. She had seen beautiful, brightly coloured lands beyond her own imagination. But this . . . this was . . . different.

It was still a dreary, brown tunnel. However, next to the door, a thick rope was fastened to the wall, and it stretched out deep into the darkness of the tunnel, further than Ember could see. Strung along the rope were cube-shaped baskets, like those at the bottom of hot air balloons. The baskets hovered inches from the muddy floor below.

'Eurgh!' shouted Hans as they stepped towards the first basket. 'It's a bit boggy.' With effort, he pulled his feet up and tried to walk forwards, the mud sticking to him with every step.

Ember could feel it too. The ground seemed to be sucking them in.

'What are the baskets for?' she wondered aloud.

'Carrying things?' suggested Hans.

Ember pulled the first one along the rope slightly. It was enormous, big enough for a person.

'Do you think they might be for carrying . . . people?' she asked. Hans shrugged, and hopped right over the side of the one closest to him, landing in the centre of the basket. Ember climbed over the straw wall to join him and tumbled to the bottom. 'Falcon, get in.'

'I'm not getting in that!' he said, a nervous laugh escaping.

Ember ignored him, eyeing the ropes. 'Do we have to pull ourselves along?' she wondered.

'Ember . . .' said Falcon, his eyes on the ground beneath the basket. 'Should *that* be happening?'

Ember looked over the side, where the mud below seemed to be . . . bubbling.

It frothed up, gurgling higher and higher until it reached the bottom of their basket. Beneath her feet, Ember felt the woven floor shift slightly. Before she had another moment to think about it, the ground itself lurched forwards, pulling their basket with them.

'Quickly!' she shouted to Falcon, holding out a hand. 'Get in!'

She pulled Falcon into the basket headfirst – and only just in time.

The basket began to gather speed, until it was hurtling along the rope. Ember clung to the side as the air whooshed in her ears.

'This doesn't make sense!' called Ember. 'It seems like . . . the ground is moving us!'

'How is that even possible?' Falcon shouted.

Hans said nothing. He was cowering in the corner, and had turned a shade of green. 'Ground-sick,' he moaned, pulling his arms across his stomach.

But before long, they were slowing down.

'I think we're arriving,' said Ember.

Clambering out of the basket, they tumbled to the floor in a heap in front of another door.

It was the same dark red wood as the ticket door. It had no handle but a rectangular letterbox-shaped panel at eye-height. Beneath it was the familiar symbol, and the words *Knock three times*.

Ember scrambled to her feet and hurried over. She knocked three times – before Hans leapt forward and rapped his own fist on the door once. 'One for good luck!' he said, looking much less green now they were out of the basket.

Immediately, the letterbox panel opened, and a pair of eyes underneath two huge bushy brown brows stared back at them.

'Can't you count?' a deep voice asked.

'Sorry,' said Ember. 'We just—'

'You're not welcome,' said the voice.

'But we—'

'No tourists.'

'We're not tourists!' Ember said, feeling a little annoyed now. 'My name's Ember Shadows. I need to talk to someone about—'

'Shadows?' The eyes studied her for a second, then drifted down to examine Hans. Ember tried to appear confident.

The letterbox closed.

For a moment, nothing happened. Ember opened her mouth, not sure what to do or say, when suddenly, the door slid upwards.

'Enter,' said the voice.

Ember swallowed and looked at Hans, who gave

her a tiny nod. With Falcon following nervously behind, they stepped through, into the darkness.

The door slammed down behind them and a light switched on above to reveal a small room with a wooden floor. One wall was entirely covered in buttons from the floor to the ceiling, and a second was made from glass with a metal rail across it. The other two, including the door-wall they had come through, were made of a silvery grey metal.

'This is a lift,' breathed Ember. She had never been in one before, but she'd read about them in her invention books.

'Where is the person who was talking to us?' whispered Hans.

They were nowhere to be seen.

'They can't have disappeared,' said Falcon. 'It doesn't make—'

But a crackle interrupted him.

'Ember Shadows?' said an old, deep voice. 'What on earth are you doing here?'

Ember looked around, not sure where to direct her voice. 'Erm . . . we have something to tell you about Mount Never. We need some help.'

Another crackle, a click, and the voice coughed softly. 'Push the button that says *Top S.E.C.R.E.T.*' Then the voice added, 'Level 1 S.E.C.R.E.T. agents to the top floor. NOW.'

The voice crackled, hissed, and was gone.

Ember turned to the wall of buttons and began to search for the right one. She could see all kinds of intriguing labels: *Mysteries to be Solved*, *No Longer Hush Hush*, *Creatures and Features of S.E.C.R.E.T. Interest* and *Inventions of the S.H.U.S.H.* But eventually, she found the one that simply read *Top S.E.C.R.E.T.*

She pressed it and an orange glow surrounded the button. A moment later, the lift shot upwards. Ember grabbed hold of the metal rail and Hans gripped her leg as they surged higher, light flooding the space through the glass wall.

As they rose, Ember realised they were in an enormous building. The lift cut right through the centre of it, the glass wall giving them a perfect view of each level as they zoomed past.

'Wow!' whispered Hans, enthralled as they sped past a room full of people with orange caps bending over an enormous book, and another where two people in long white coats seemed to be experimenting with beakers of inky-looking fluid. Every room they saw was different. Ember gasped longingly as they rose level with one filled with piles and piles of metal gears, cogs, bolts and screws. The lift slowed and Ember saw an old man stood among the piles, twisting a metal thread around a piece of machinery. He looked up, one eye magnified by a glass contraption strapped to his head.

Ember met the man's gaze. She'd never seen someone who looked so much like an inventor.

A *real* inventor.

'I don't like this place,' muttered Falcon.

With a jolt that sent Ember stumbling, the lift pulled sideways. Rooms and rooms of exciting things flew by and Ember gazed at them hungrily until her view was blocked by a black screen that appeared over the glass wall, with the words NO LOOKING. S.E.C.R.E.T.

'Isn't it *all* secret?' asked Hans.

'I guess some bits are more secret than others,' said Ember.

As quickly as it had started, the lift came to a stop, a high-pitched *ding* announcing its arrival.

The silvery grey wall behind them slid upwards, revealing what Ember assumed was the *Top S.E.C.R.E.T.* room.

They stepped out to find one man sitting at the end of a long, oval-shaped table.

The room was surrounded on all sides by tall mahogany bookshelves, packed with thick books that looked as though they had been there for centuries. The man at the end, with his white hair and walking stick, his black suit and wrinkled face, seemed to fit in perfectly among the old books.

Slowly, he got to his feet and began to walk around the table towards them.

Ember's heart started to hammer. Maybe Falcon was right; they should have told someone what they were planning. She had no idea what she had gotten them all into.

'Jasper Clay,' said the man, holding out his hand. 'Director of S.E.C.R.E.T. A pleasure to meet you.'

Ember bravely stepped forwards, Hans clinging to her leg from behind. She shook Jasper's thin hand.

'Ember Shadows,' she said.

'Oh I know who you are,' he said, and crouched down to meet Hans. 'And you too, sir. Hans, isn't it? A real pleasure.'

Hans looked up at Ember with delight, releasing her leg. 'Sir?' he said, his eyes wide. 'No one's ever called me "sir" before. Ember, this place is *great!*'

Jasper smiled. Hans shook Jasper's forefinger vigorously.

Ember smiled cautiously. He seemed nice enough . . .

'But you,' said Jasper, turning to Falcon, 'I don't have the pleasure of knowing you yet.'

Falcon looked to the floor but held out his hand. 'I'm Falcon. Just Falcon.'

Ember frowned. She didn't know anyone except Hans who had one name. But it didn't seem to bother Jasper.

'A pleasure, Falcon,' he said. 'Please, all of you take a seat. A few S.E.C.R.E.T. agents will be joining us momentarily. Before they do, why don't you tell me why you're here?'

'We have an emergency,' Ember said. 'And we're hoping you might be able to help.'

They sat at the table and Ember explained everything as quickly as she could: her part in destroying the Fate Cards, the difficulty everyone was having in making decisions now, the spiders, the muddy footprints, and finally, the threads being cut.

When she had finished, Jasper closed his eyes and leaned back in his chair.

Ember's shoulders loosened a little as the weight of

the story lifted from her. Jasper was going to help, she was sure of it. This was a secret society, dedicated to the protection of magical landscapes. If anyone could help, it was S.E.C.R.E.T. Surely this was exactly what they were created to do!

Finally, everything was going to be OK . . .

She waited with bated breath for Jasper to speak. 'My dear,' he said, his voice shaking. 'This is worse than we could have possibly imagined.'

7

As Ember reeled from Jasper's words, the door to the lift slid open, and a woman stepped into the room.

The woman, who had dark brown skin and straight, glimmering, silver hair, nodded briefly at Ember, Hans and Falcon, before taking a seat next to Jasper.

'Anise, welcome,' said Jasper. 'This is Anise Miller, one of our top agents.'

'What's going on?' she asked. She wrung her hands together, her eyes flickering between the two children and Hans.

'Are the others coming?' asked Jasper.

Anise shook her head. 'Topaz is preparing to visit the Tremoring Tropics, and May is at the Emotion right now.'

What are the Tremoring Tropics and the Emotion? wondered Ember, briefly distracted by the possibility of other magical landscapes.

'Well then, we'd better get started,' Jasper said.

'We have an emergency. It is time for Operation Never Ever.'

Anise gasped. 'You can't be serious!'

'I'm afraid I am. Ember comes bearing bad news,' Jasper said gravely. 'Someone has been cutting threads on Mount Never.'

'No . . .' said Anise softly. 'No, it can't be!'

'Wait, I don't understand,' said Ember.

'What's Operation Never Ever?' asked Falcon.

Jasper turned to them and smiled. 'Apologies, we've gotten ahead of ourselves. We'd better explain from the beginning. Anise, the map, please.'

Anise rose from her seat and pulled out an enormous rolled parchment from a hidden drawer under the table. With some trouble, she removed the string keeping it together and let it roll out, from one end of the table all the way to the other.

The map was truly magnificent. The shapes of countries and islands and oceans filled the map from left to right, covered with tiny illustrations: snow-capped peaks, minuscule roads and railways, boats crossing the sea. Ember wanted to run her fingers over the fields, the rivers, the incredible mountains.

Jasper pulled a black rod from his pocket and extended one end, a long silver pointer emerging from the top. He reached across the map to the northern-most part and pointed at a small green speck on the map, surrounded by mountains.

'This,' he said, 'is Everspring.'

For a moment, Ember thought she must have misunderstood. He had pointed to such a tiny village, no bigger than the size of her nail, on a map that stretched right across the table. She had known there was a whole world out there, but never had she expected it to be so . . . well, so *enormous*.

'Sorry, Mr Jasper, but you've got it wrong,' said Hans, jumping up on to the table and peering down at the tiny picture of Everspring. 'There's no *way* that could be Everspring, it's too small. In Everspring, we've got houses, a river, a school, a tree house, shops, and—'

'Oh but it *is* Everspring,' Jasper interrupted with a small smile. 'Everspring is a remarkably small village. Now, *here* is Mount Never,' he said, jabbing a large mountain illustration above Everspring. 'And *here* is S.E.C.R.E.T. HQ, where we are now.' He jabbed the exact centre of the map.

'But that journey would have taken us days,' Ember said.

Anise leaned forward, smiling for the first time. 'But it didn't, thanks to my basket invention!' she said. 'Did you enjoy it?'

Ember opened her mouth to respond, but Jasper spoke first.

'Mount Never creates the Threads of Fate for this entire quarter of the world,' he said. Looking closer, Ember realised the map was divided into four; two diagonal, dotted lines split the map, crossing at the centre to form an X. Jasper traced the northern quarter, an upturned triangle, with his pointer. Most of the world within it was blue ocean; only a small amount was covered in green land. 'Moira was controlling all of these people's fates.'

MOUNT WHEN

'What about everyone in the rest of the map?' asked Hans.

'There are three other Fate Mountains, similar to Mount Never. Here, we have Mount Ever.' He pointed to the east of the map. 'Mount Sometimes, in the south. And Mount When, in the west.'

'N. E. S. W.,' muttered Ember. The letters around the outside of the S.E.C.R.E.T. symbol; they were both points on a compass *and* the first letter of the names of the four Fate Mountains.

'Each mountain creates the Threads of Fate for people living in its quarter. Do you understand?' said Jasper.

Ember, Falcon and Hans nodded. Hans walked over the map as if he were a giant.

'But the mountains and their realms are not the only magical landscapes,' said Jasper.

Excitement exploded within Ember as Jasper confirmed her hopes. *Ms Daylands was right.* 'What are the other landscapes?' she asked eagerly.

'We don't have time to discuss them now,' said Jasper. Then he saw Ember's disappointed face and gave in. 'I suppose I can tell you about a few. The biggest one is the Emotion.'

Ember frowned. 'Emotion?' she said.

'Not Em*otion*,' he said, and drew his pointer across the sea that spanned the map, before coming to a stop on a row of small, neat letters: *Emocean*. He tapped the word twice and looked at Ember. 'Em*ocean*. This ocean provides the world's emotions. We try as best we can to keep it calm. The last thing you'd want is a tidal wave of sorrow lapping up on the border of your village, or a tsunami of fear.'

Ember couldn't even imagine it . . . an ocean that created feelings? It seemed too vast to capture in her mind.

'We also have the Tremoring Tropics, where weather is formed.' Jasper tapped a jungle-like area of the map.

A jungle of weather, Ember thought. *How does that work?* She looked down at Hans, whose eyes were wide with wonder.

Jasper was moving on, and Ember's thoughts of raining plants and flowers filled with sunshine faded away.

'And we also have the Lost Desert of Time,' added

Jasper, pulling his pointer away, and pushing it closed. 'The desert watches over time itself and is one of our biggest mysteries. It's rumoured to have the power to stop time, or even turn it back. Imagine that!'

'Where is it?' said Hans, looking for a desert on the map.

'It's lost,' explained Ember, understanding that at least.

'How can a desert be lost?' asked Falcon, his eyes also scanning the map.

'Simple. No one has seen it for centuries,' said Jasper. 'That's not all of the landscapes, but we must move on.'

Ember couldn't take her eyes away from the map. A lost magical desert? A jungle that formed the weather itself? She had always thought there *must* be more magic to the world than Mount Never alone – but *this* much?

'Mr Jasper,' said Hans softly. 'In the whole world, in any of these landscapes, is there anyone else like me?'

'Not that I know of, sir,' said Jasper. 'Magical creatures, yes. But no one quite like you. You are unique.'

Hans nodded, but Ember could see disappointment in his face.

'You still haven't told us what Operation Never Ever is,' said Falcon.

'Not yet, no,' said Jasper. He sighed. 'I was getting there. But I'm afraid you're not going to like this, not one bit.'

8

Ember's stomach knotted tighter.

'At S.E.C.R.E.T., our job is to protect *all* the magical landscapes,' said Jasper. 'To do so, an agent is assigned to each one. Moira was assigned to look after Mount Never.'

'She didn't really *look after* it,' said Hans.

'You're right, Mr Hans,' said Jasper with an apologetic smile. 'By the time we knew that she had been controlling the mountain, it was too late. The society agreed that getting rid of Moira would expose the ability to control a landscape, and *that* was a very dangerous thing.'

'So you just . . . left her?' said Ember.

'*I* didn't,' said Jasper. 'I'm not *that* old, my dear, it was a hundred years ago. But yes, S.E.C.R.E.T. did.' He sighed again, heavily. 'Moira was only able to reach the threads that came from Mount Never. So, we kept your quarter of the world secluded from the rest. We helped spread Moira's rumours about how stepping foot on the mountain would wipe away your fate. We did everything we could to keep Moira's control over the mountain a secret. After all, she was creating balance. When you consider how the mountain *could* have been abused, she wasn't doing too much wrong.'

Ember glared at the map and the tiny dot that represented Everspring. Maybe in the grand scheme of the world it wasn't that much, but in *her* village and any others in the northern quarter, real people's lives were affected, cut short or changed, all because S.E.C.R.E.T. had thought it better to keep quiet about what was going on. Anger bubbled inside her.

'However, we always knew there might come a day when Moira was stopped,' Jasper continued. 'When the ability to control a landscape was exposed.'

'Which is what you did,' said Anise quietly, 'when you freed everyone from the Fate Cards.'

'Exactly. And now someone has also found their way on to Mount Never and cut threads,' said Jasper gravely. 'But we have been preparing for something like this for many years. Which is where Operation Never Ever comes in.'

Anise leaned forwards and pointed to a drawing of three clouds over the top of a small island in the western quarter of the map. 'I look after this magical landscape: Cloud Memory,' she said. 'It's where all memories are stored. The cloud moves around the world, picking up memories every second of every day. If you've forgotten something, it's because it's no longer in the cloud.'

Ember gazed at Anise admiringly. This woman was a leader in a secret organisation, looking after all the memories of the whole world. And she was an inventor!

'Cloud Memory holds all the memories in the world?' Falcon asked as he leaned in closer to the map.

'That's right,' Anise said. 'Which is why it's the key to fixing this mess. I'll catch up with Cloud Memory and retrieve all the memories of Moira. I'll destroy them, along with everyone's memories related to the Fate Cards and the Threads of Fate. That way no one, not even the Thread-Cutter, will remember that the mountains can be controlled.'

Anise leaned back in her chair, folded her arms, and smiled.

'And then the Fate Mountains and the rest of the

magical landscapes will be safe, for ever,' she said.

'But wiping people's memories . . .' stammered Falcon. 'Isn't that a bit . . . drastic?'

'Wait,' Ember said, trying to gather her thoughts. 'If you destroy all the memories, no one will even remember that they had a card in the first place?'

'That's right,' said Jasper. 'Whatever their lives are like right now, people will believe that they *chose* them the whole time. It will be as if Moira never set foot on Mount Never.'

The memory of everything Ember had done would be erased. No one would be angry at her any more, and the mountain would be safe . . .

'You can't do that!' Falcon burst out.

'We must,' said Jasper, frowning. 'We'll be saving lives.'

Hans reached out for Ember's knee. 'What about us?' he asked, looking up at her.

Jasper coughed awkwardly. 'Unfortunately, Ember, your memory would be affected too. You wouldn't remember your journey up Mount Never. That would include anyone you met there.'

Hans.

Ember thought she might be sick. Lose all her memories of Hans? 'No,' she whispered, barely audible.

Hans began to sob, clinging to her jacket.

'Hans,' continued Jasper, looking concerned. 'We aren't sure how all this will affect you. We believe your memories will remain intact, but Ember's won't.'

'No,' Ember repeated. 'I won't let this happen.'

'Anise, you'll need to go today,' said Jasper quietly, turning to her. 'There's not a moment to lose.'

Anise nodded. 'If I head to the cloud now, it will be done by tomorrow.'

'So tomorrow,' said Hans, stammering between

sobs, 'tomorrow, Ember won't remember me?'

Jasper nodded solemnly. 'I'm afraid so,' he murmured.

Hans collapsed into another bout of tears.

How can this be happening? thought Ember. Hans was her best friend. They had been through so much together and she was just going to . . . forget him?

'If there was another way . . .' said Jasper.

But Ember wasn't listening. She was scanning the map, searching for another idea, another way to stop the Thread-Cutter. It wasn't fair. Lose her best friend? The memory of what had happened? Of Florence, the magical realms, even learning the truth about her dad's sacrifice for her?

Jasper continued. 'I know it feels as though all hope is lost, but—'

'Lost!' Ember screamed, the word bursting from her. 'That's it!'

The room fell silent. All eyes were on her as her mind spun furiously.

'The Lost Desert of *Time*,' she said. 'You said it controls time, yes?'

Jasper frowned. 'Yes, but—'

'How?' Ember said.

'No one knows,' said Jasper with a shrug. But Ember was already on to her next thought.

'If its job is to control time, then who knows what it can do,' she said. 'Maybe the rumours are true, maybe there *is* a way to turn time backwards. We could catch whoever is cutting the threads *before* they did it. We could save the threads, *and* everyone could be allowed to remember the Fate Cards.' A small voice in her head told her this wouldn't stop another person from cutting or manipulating Fate Threads in the future, but she stomped that thought down. She would deal with that later.

Jasper shook his head. 'Ember, the desert is *lost*. There's not a person alive who has seen it. The legends say the only way to find it is with all four Fate Mountain maps, and—'

'Fate Mountain maps?' said Ember. Her thoughts were racing, the way they did whenever she had the sparks of an idea. If she could just bring the right sparks together, she knew they could erupt into a blazing plan.

Anise and Jasper exchanged a glance of exasperation.

'The maps to the Fate Mountains,' said Jasper. 'They show all the hidden tunnels of each mountain, and, used together, they supposedly show the route to the desert. But we only have two of the four Fate Mountain maps: the Sometimes Map, and the When Map. We have no idea where the other two are. And even if by some miracle we found them, we'd then need to search for the desert. We don't have time for this. A Thread-Cutter is on the loose! We can't stand idly by while—'

But Ember was already pulling the map of Mount Never from her bag. 'Is this one of the Fate Mountain maps?'

In unison, Anise and Jasper's eyes widened.

'Well, yes,' said Jasper, examining it in disbelief. '*That* is the Never Map. But without the fourth map, the Ever Map, you'll *never* find the desert.'

'Then let us find the fourth map,' said Falcon. 'We . . . we have to.'

Ember looked at him and offered a small smile of thanks. She hadn't expected his support.

'We've been searching for it for years. We've scoured every inch of Mount Ever. As it's not there,

there's no way of knowing where it could be,' said Jasper, becoming more and more agitated.

'We need to try,' said Ember. 'And I know it's the right thing to—'

'Can you *really* trust your own judgement?' asked Jasper suddenly. 'Didn't you trust Moira when she *lured* you up the mountain in the first place?'

His words hit Ember in the stomach like a punch. She glared back at him, holding his stare as she felt her cheeks redden.

Finally, Anise broke the silence. 'Jasper, with three maps, finding the fourth might be possible. The legends say the maps work together—'

'An old fairy tale is hardly enough instruction to send a group of *children* off to find the final map!' Jasper shouted.

Hans leapt on to the table. 'Ember was a child when she stopped Moira. *You're* an adult but you never could.'

Jasper's face softened. He gave a tiny nod to Hans and sank back into his chair. 'You're right,' he said. 'Ember, I'm sorry for my outburst. It's just, this whole situation is . . . impossible.'

'Let us try,' Ember said. 'If we find the fourth map, the Ever Map, we might be able to find the desert.'

'Even if you do,' said Jasper, 'we don't know that turning back time is possible. And if it *is*, it would be dangerous. If you meddle with time, you meddle with every single landscape – the fabric of our world would begin to unravel. It would be like pulling a loose thread on a jumper; very soon, you'd have nothing left. You could only turn it back for a short time or the consequences could be disastrous.'

'We wouldn't need long,' pleaded Ember, remembering what Florence had said. 'The threads *definitely* weren't cut the midnight before last.'

'A day might be safe enough,' said Anise slowly. 'No more than two.'

Jasper began to tap the table, his fingers drumming out an anxious rhythm as he thought.

Ember saw a small antique clock nestled in the bookshelves behind Anise. *Midday*. It had been a day and a half since the threads were cut. If they had two days at the most to turn back time and lie in wait to catch the Thread-Cutter, they would have to do it by midnight, tonight! Which meant . . .

'Give us twelve hours to find the Ever Map and the desert,' she pleaded. 'If we *can* turn back time, we will do so exactly two days and then wait for the Thread-Cutter and catch them before they do anything.'

She paused and drew a deep breath. 'If we haven't done it by midnight, you can go to Cloud Memory and take everyone's memories.'

Neither Jasper nor Anise said a word. As the silence grew, Hans grabbed Ember's thumb and squeezed. She felt Falcon tense beside her. All three of them waited, staring at Jasper.

'Right,' said Jasper, clapping his hands together and checking his watch. 'I'll give you a total of *six* hours to find the Ever Map. After that, you report back here. Understand? Then we'll have six hours left to go to the desert together and try your plan.' He paused. 'One way or another, by midnight, this *will* be behind us.'

Despite the terrifyingly short time they had, Ember could have cheered. Hans did.

He leapt from Ember's lap and zoomed around their heads, whooping as he went. A smile lit up Falcon's face.

'Let me warn you,' said Jasper. 'When I said you'll have six hours, I meant six of our *normal* hours, but time will get away from you in the magical landscapes, it doesn't work the same there. Take this,' he said, removing his watch from his wrist. He handed it to Falcon while Ember rolled up the Never Map. 'It will adjust to the flow of time in each landscape to show how much time is passing here at S.E.C.R.E.T., so you'll have an accurate countdown.'

'Thank you,' said Falcon as he strapped it to his wrist.

'And you will need the other maps,' said Jasper. Anise stood and turned to one of the mahogany bookshelves behind her. She pulled on a shelf and to Ember's surprise, it opened like a secret drawer. Carefully, Anise reached in and pulled out two long tubes.

'These are the Sometimes and When Maps,' said Anise, handing them to Ember. 'We don't know exactly how they work to show the way to the desert. The legends refer to them *pointing to one another*.'

Ember placed them into her bag as carefully as she could.

'If you haven't returned in six hours with the Ever Map,' said Jasper, 'Anise will go to Cloud Memory.'

Ember nodded, then turned and made for the lift, Hans on her shoulder. They didn't have a second to spare. Falcon stumbled over his chair, pushed his hair back from his face, and followed her. Ember jabbed the button and waited for it to arrive.

'Go to the ticket booth in the Main Hall,' said Anise. 'You'll need All-Access-Passes so that you can use the network of S.E.C.R.E.T. tunnels around the world.'

'Thank you,' Ember said. *A network of tunnels around the world?* The scale of what she had decided to do was beginning to overwhelm her. Finally, the wall slid up to reveal the inside of the elevator.

'Good luck to all three of you,' called Jasper.

They were going to need it, Ember realised.

Because, as the doors closed, she realised she hadn't got a clue where to start.

9

'Whoopeee!' shouted Hans as Ember pushed a button that read *Main Hall*. The lift surged. 'We did it!'

He bounced over to Falcon, who took a step back, apparently still a bit unsure of Hans.

'And you helped us!' said Hans. 'That means you can officially be our friend.'

Ember gave Falcon a half-smile. 'Thanks for backing us up in there,' she said. 'I was a bit surprised though. Most people want to forget all about the Fate Cards.'

Falcon frowned for a second, and then shrugged. 'I guess so. I just thought it wasn't right to forget what you and Moira did to everyone along with them.'

Ember opened her mouth to defend herself. She had never meant for any of this to happen; surely *she* shouldn't be lumped in with Moira? But arguing with Falcon wouldn't do any good now, so instead she turned to the window and watched as the insides of

S.E.C.R.E.T. sailed past.

'You never told us your other name,' said Hans, ignoring the awkward silence. 'Ember is Ember *Shadows*. I'm just Hans, but I thought all humans had two names, like Ember.'

'I don't have another name, not any more,' Falcon said.

'Why not?' asked Ember. 'Everyone has a surname—'

'What are those things on your feet?' Falcon interrupted, pointing at Hans.

'Shh!-Oos,' said Hans proudly. 'Ember invented them. They stop your feet from making any noise when you walk!'

Falcon didn't look impressed. 'Not half as cool as what Jasper gave me. A watch that can monitor the flow of time anywhere in the world.'

'He didn't give it to *you*, he gave it to *us*,' said Ember, bristling. 'Anyway, you didn't explain—'

'We've got six hours, right?' Falcon said, ignoring her as he fiddled with the watch. Ember saw that it had lots of different hands on it, each one spinning in its own rhythm. 'Now, how does this thing work?'

'Be careful,' Ember said, worried by his fierce jabbing at the watch.

'I'm trying to set a timer,' he said. He pushed one of the buttons on the side, and a high-pitched beeping sound came from the watch. 'There, done.'

'Great,' said Ember, without enthusiasm. She was happy they had a way to track the countdown, but she didn't like how smug he sounded.

'I was thinking,' said Falcon. 'Why don't we go and ask Ms Daylands and Haywood for some help finding the Ever Map?'

'I told you before, we don't have time for to argue with them!' said Ember.

'Fine,' he said coldly. 'Then I assume you have a plan? Where are we starting?'

'I . . . I haven't got that far yet,' Ember muttered. Her own map had been found on Mount Never, but Jasper had already searched Mount Ever for the fourth map, so it couldn't be there. She had no idea where they should begin.

'What?' said Falcon, his eyebrows raised. 'Then we *have* to talk to the adults about this! Otherwise you may as well kiss your memories goodbye.'

Hans let out a giggle. 'You can't kiss memories,' he said. 'Not even really good ones. Anyway, Ember and I are *fantastic* at finding things, and we're a brilliant team. We can figure it out on our own. Right, Ember Shadows?'

Ember smiled bleakly; she didn't want to admit that a plague of doubts was worming through her body.

It was beginning to dawn on her that, once again, she'd made a huge decision that would affect not just everyone in Everspring, but the whole world. And this time it wasn't to save her sister, it was to save the lives of strangers and her friendship with Hans and their memories of Mount Never. It was an awfully big responsibility.

'We can do this,' she said firmly. 'The first step is getting the passes.'

The lift came to a halt and a rumble-mix of chatter and feet spread towards them as the door slid open and revealed the Main Hall.

The room was like a tunnel of its own. The back wall, which stretched out to the left and right as far as Ember could see, was lined with different coloured doors. People she could only assume were S.E.C.R.E.T. agents were bustling around, their shoes clacking against the glistening black and white tiled floor. Despite the number of people around, the enormous room was immaculate. Every inch seemed to gleam and glow; even the air smelt fresh, as though they were on the surface rather than hundreds of feet below ground.

Where are they all going? wondered Ember, wishing for a moment that they had more time to explore S.E.C.R.E.T. HQ. But as she watched, she saw agents stepping through the doorways. Each door had a blackboard sign above it, with white letters showing its destination. Some were room names Ember recognised from buttons in the lift, others were tunnel entrances to landscapes Jasper hadn't mentioned, like *Broken Heart Hotspring*, and *Natural Wonders Woodland*. Straight ahead, a tall, freestanding blackboard listed even more destinations, including *Mount Never*.

A crackle erupted somewhere above them, followed by a hiss and a high-pitched whistle as the microphone adjusted. Ember covered her ears but no one else seemed bothered by it.

Then, a voice broke through. 'The tunnel to the Luck's All Mine has now been repaired and is ready for use.'

She glanced down at Hans next to her, who was hopping from one foot to the other, seemingly thrilled by the sight of so many people.

With a defiant punch into the air, he stepped forwards. 'Let's get those passes.'

'But *then* where will we go?' Falcon asked impatiently. 'There's no point in getting passes unless we know where we're going.'

All around them, the hum of busy S.E.C.R.E.T. agents continued.

Ember tried to block it out so she could think. Falcon was right, they needed to figure out where they would search first.

Jasper and Anise had said the maps *pointed to one another* somehow, according to an old myth. So maybe one of the maps themselves *might* help them decide where to go.

'Let's take a closer look at the maps. Maybe there will be a clue,' she said. The three of them moved out of the way of the crowd, and Ember handed them each a map. She unfurled the Never Map herself and spread it on the floor in front of them.

Each of them studied a map, their noses nearly touching the paper.

'Nothing,' said Falcon, once they had exhausted every inch. 'What about on the back?'

But the backs were empty.

Ember sat up. 'Maybe it's something that *isn't* there . . .' she murmured, the cogs turning in her mind. 'A message in invisible ink, or something hidden within the paper?'

She glanced around. Windows in the high ceiling above let in bright light, and she held up the map against the glare to see if it revealed anything. Nothing.

Then, she carefully took her bottle of water and wet her hands. Ever so gently, she dampened the edge of the Never Map, hoping the water might reveal some hidden message. Still nothing.

Hans slumped to the floor with a sigh. 'If only we knew more about the legends.'

'Didn't Ms Daylands say there was a book about them?' asked Falcon thoughtfully.

'Of course! Hans!' shouted Ember.

'What?' Hans asked with a blank stare. 'I've never written a book.'

'No,' she laughed. 'Hans Christof Sanderson!'

Hans' face lit up as he realised what she meant. 'Yes! I remember!'

'Would you two *please* stop talking in riddles!' said Falcon.

'We found his book in the Know-It-Hall on Mount Never,' said Hans.

'Know-It-Hall?' asked Falcon, looking even more confused now.

'Enormous hall of knowledge on Mount Never,' said Ember. 'Lots of books.'

'So?' asked Falcon.

'So, Ms Daylands said Hans Christof Sanderson's book was a collection of stories about the magical landscapes. We go to the Know-It-Hall, find the book again, and see if there's any more information about the legends and the maps in there,' explained Ember. 'They might give us a clue as to how these maps work together.'

'Your plan is to go to a big library to find a book that *might* tell you more about the maps,' said Falcon. 'That's *it*?'

120

'Unless you have a better idea?' she asked, staring back at him.

He sighed, shook his head, and then thrust his map towards her. 'Let's go then.'

Ember leapt to her feet and the familiar butterflies started to dance in her stomach. It wasn't really a plan, not entirely. But sometimes, the beginnings of a plan are all that's needed. At least, she hoped so.

'Let's get those passes and get to Everspring,' she said, trying her best to sound confident.

She put the three maps away and led the way down the busy hall, weaving between all kinds of people, looking for a ticket booth that would give them the All-Access-Passes.

Eventually, Falcon called out. 'There!' he said, as he spotted it, a single white booth with the sign *Tickets* in large black letters above.

The three of them ran to the window, where a short man with a dark blue hat sat, slumped over the desk, his head buried in his hands.

Ember coughed gently. 'Excuse me,' she said.

The man woke with a start and looked up. 'What?' he asked gruffly.

'We need three All-Access-Passes, please,' she said.

'Names?' he said, clicking his fingers.

'Ember Shadows, Hans, and . . . Falcon,' said Ember.

She was beginning to feel like the strange one having two names.

The man looked up from his register and narrowed his eyes. '*You've* been cleared for all-access?'

Ember nodded.

'But how?' said the man, his eyes now wide and curious. 'You're not even agents!'

'It's a long story and we're in a bit of a hurry,' said Falcon.

The man deflated and sighed. 'Fine,' he said, handing over three tickets.

These were much more exciting than the tickets they had found in Moira's train. They were larger – a similar size to a Fate Card. It was a holographic material, and across the front the network of tunnels was carefully drawn, their lines criss-crossing like a web. Each way Ember tilted the card revealed different lines.

Never Baskets Line 417. Tropics Tree Log Line 312. Emocean Walkalater Line 21. FUNicular Line 981.

At the end of each line was a circle, with a destination written above: *Tremoring Tropics*, *Mount Never*, *Emocean* . . .

Ember shivered. The Fate Card, the network, the strange names for the lines – everywhere around her she saw bits of Moira.

The Fateweaver had obviously been inspired by her time at S.E.C.R.E.T. when she made the train for the Messy Middle, and the machine on top of the mountain.

'Wait,' she said, turning back to the ticket officer. 'How do we find the entrances to the tunnels?'

The man stared back as if she was asking the most obvious question in the world. 'You follow your nose of course,' he said.

'But I don't have a nose!' cried Hans.

'Not *nose*,' said the man with an impatient sigh. 'N.O.S.E. The Navigational Object for Secret Entrances; it's built into your ticket. The circle at the end of each line is a button. You simply tap the circle of the destination you want, and a light will begin to flash at the end of your ticket. Hold the ticket out ahead of you and move it around. It will flash faster when you're facing the right direction and slow down whenever you're getting off track.'

'Thank you,' said Ember, studying her ticket. *How had someone packed so much into such a small thing?* She would have to take it apart to learn more about how it had been invented . . . if they made it through this mess. 'What about the tunnel from here to Mount Never?' she asked, realising she wasn't sure how to get back to where they had entered S.E.C.R.E.T. 'Where is that?'

'Take the lift and press the button for *Never This Way*,' he said.

Ember thanked him again and turned back to find Falcon was already striding across the hall to the elevator.

'I thought we were in a hurry?' he called back.

Hans and Ember exchanged a glance, and Ember saw her own mixed-up emotions reflected back at her.

They could do this.

Tickets in hand, they set off for the lift and the tunnel that would take them back to Everspring – and on to the next stage of their journey.

10

As they emerged from the tunnel, Ember saw Florence sitting where they had left her, perched on a rock ahead.

'Oh Ember, thank goodness,' she said, swooping down to meet them. 'Did you find anything?'

'We did,' said Ember. 'But it's not good.'

As quickly as she could, Ember explained all they had learnt.

'So, you're off to find a book about the legends?' asked Florence. 'Don't you think you should tell Ms Daylands?'

'That's what I said,' said Falcon.

'She wouldn't let us go,' said Ember. 'She told me we had to spend time *planning* instead of *doing*. Well, we don't have time for that.'

Florence looked over her glasses. 'Shouldn't you tell *someone* where you're going?'

'I'll go,' said Falcon. 'I need to speak to Haywood anyway . . . I need to—'

'Why am I the only one who sees how awful this is!' shouted Ember suddenly. 'We only have six hours! Every minute matters!'

No one said a word.

'Ember's right,' Hans said at last. At least she could count on Hans.

'What if we sent a letter?' suggested Falcon. 'That will only take a second. Haywood will be worried about me . . . and what about your mum and your sister?'

Ember softened slightly. 'Fine,' she conceded. 'You write it. Tell him we're safe, but you *can't* tell him what we're doing. He'll tell Ms Daylands and they'll only try and stop us.'

She pulled the Never Map from her bag and began searching for the tunnel to take them to the Know-It-Hall. Falcon wrote a note, folded it up, and passed it to Florence.

'I'll come and find you once I've delivered it,' Florence said to Ember. 'Someone needs to keep an eye on you.'

Ember nodded stiffly and kept her eyes on the map. 'We'll be in the Know-It-Hall.'

Following the map, she walked slightly off the path

to a large flat stone on the ground. With effort, she pushed it aside to reveal an opening in the earth.

'Are you sure about this?' said Falcon, watching but, Ember thought crossly, doing nothing to help.

She ignored him, lowered herself into the tunnel and then dropped down. A quick shake of her Illumitube lit the space ahead. Hans bounced down, followed by Falcon.

They began walking.

'Why is *this* tunnel just a tunnel,' said Hans, 'but all the ones at S.E.C.R.E.T. have strange names and transport?'

'I'm not sure,' said Ember. 'Maybe because this tunnel only goes between the realms of Mount Never, which is a single magical landscape. The other ones go all over the world *between* lots of different magical landscapes.'

They hurried along the narrow tunnel until Falcon stopped suddenly, paused for a moment, and sniffed. 'What's that smell?' he said.

Ember took a deep breath, the scent of old paper and leather mixing with the fresh smell of the mountain's grass.

Hans took one short inhale and broke into an enormous grin.

'BOOKS!' he yelled, bouncing ahead of them to the tunnel end. There, at the edge, was the back of a bookshelf.

'It's a bit of a squeeze,' warned Ember as she carefully inched her way around its edge, breathing in as best she could, until she popped out the other side.

Despite the moody bookworms who occupied it, this was still Ember's favourite realm.

Thousands of books filled the tall, high bookcases. Others, flapping overhead, darted and dived among one another until they found their spot on a shelf and landed.

When Ember had last been here, it had been silent, apart from the flapping of the books. But since the Threads of Fate had been freed, the Know-It-Hall was no longer a quiet, peaceful space. Instead, hundreds of threads weaved and scurried around the room. They were everywhere, like fireworks shooting through the air. Ember could spot some curled up between books, some slithering along the floor or climbing the shelves, all thirsty to learn more. It was amazing, seeing all these threads desperate to change and move and grow, just as their owners down in the towns below read, learnt at school, or spoke to new people.

A warm feeling spread through her chest. It was the first time in a while that freeing the Threads of Fate had felt like a good idea.

'Come on then, teamerino!' shouted Hans. 'We need to find that book!'

'We should split up,' said Ember. 'Take a section each and—'

'You again. I thought I asked you not to come back.'

Ember recognised that weary, groaning voice. Sure enough, a familiar figure wriggled out from between two books on a shelf beside Hans. The first time they had visited the Know-It-Hall, the bookworm had fallen right off the shelf.

'Hi again,' said Ember to the bookworm. 'Sorry to bother you, but we wanted to know if—'

'I *really* don't have time to give you riddles today,' said the worm. 'You're the reason all these threads are here, messing up my cataloguing system. I have more than enough work to do without helping you through the realm a second time.'

'What's your name?' asked Hans.

The question, which surprised Ember, seemed to startle the bookworm too.

'My name?' she said. 'No one's ever asked me that before.' She blinked, composing herself, and stood tall on her tail. 'My name is Brontey.'

'What a super-duper name,' said Hans. 'I'm Hans.'

'Thank you,' said Brontey, straightening her skirt. 'We choose our own names from the books on the shelves. You know, we have an author here called Hans. None called Ember though. And who are you? I haven't seen you before.'

'He's Falcon,' said Ember.

'I don't know any authors named Falcon,' she said, 'but maybe one called Robi—'

'We would actually like to find the book by the author Hans,' Ember said, cutting her off. They didn't have time for her to list every author with a bird-related name. 'Can you help us?'

Brontey looked at them, narrowing her eyes. 'Why should I?'

Ember smiled, remembering bookworms and their

special weakness. 'I could bring you some more bottles of ink, if you like?'

Brontey's eyes lit up. 'Deal.' Without hesitation, she let out a low whistle. The sound was so quiet, Ember knew she wouldn't have heard it from much further away, and yet the noise seemed to reverberate around them like a tuning fork.

In response to Brontey's call, a blue hardback book appeared overhead. Its covers were spread open like wings, and its pages hung beneath as it sailed through the air straight towards them. Falcon ducked to get out of its way as it swooped up and landed open in front of Brontey. Falcon looked at Ember, stunned. But Ember simply grinned in return. She *loved* this place. The thought of forgetting it all . . .

No, she wouldn't think about that.

She turned back to Brontey, who was using her tail to sift through the pages. The blue book appeared to be some sort of catalogue.

'There we are. Hans Christof Sanderson,' she said, wriggling on to the page. 'Yes, hmm, OK, then.'

Ember peered over at the book. Next to the author's name, there were six musical notes handwritten on the page.

Brontey whistled a short tune, clearly using the notes on the page as her guide, then she waited, tapping her tail against the book. Before long, a book bird wove its way between the shelves, dived down, and landed gently beside them.

'That's amazing! You're a book whistler!' shouted

Hans, jumping up and down. 'Wowee! I wish I could whistle for books.' He made an 'ooh' shape with his mouth, but ended up blowing raspberries instead.

Brontey smiled smugly. 'It is a rather special skill,' she said.

'Thank you, Brontey,' said Ember as she reached for the chunky book. Its hard, purple cover was embossed with gold, loopy writing and the words: *Tales of Time Gone By: The Magic Beneath Our Feet. Recorded by Hans Christof Sanderson.*

Ember, Hans and Falcon sat on the floor, Threads of Fate surrounding them. Ember could hardly breathe. She tried not to think of what might happen if this book didn't have a clue.

She just hoped, prayed, wished, that there was *something*.

Ember opened the book.

She turned the pages, slowly at first, and then flicking faster as she got further into the book without seeing any sort of clue. There were dozens of stories, all sprinkled with beautiful illustrations depicting strange magical creatures or far off lands. In the corners of the pages were delicate little designs, and illustrations of vines and flowers were woven around the text. However there was no mention of the maps.

Then, halfway through the book, she came across a story titled: *The Legend of the Fate Mountains*. She paused, her heart beating faster.

'Shall I read it?' she asked.

Hans nodded, crossing his legs and resting his elbows on his knees, his chin on his hands. Falcon shrugged, but he too was leaning forward, ready to listen.

'*Long ago,*' Ember began, '*when the world was barely born, there was only Time. Time was very busy, keeping the world turning, the clocks ticking, and the sun rising. And so Time wished upon the stars above for something to help her.*'

Ember paused. She could almost feel the magic in the words.

'*Hearing her wish, the four Fate Mountains rose from the Earth, each one promising to serve the Desert of Time.*'

'He makes them sound like people,' whispered Falcon.

Ember continued reading.

'*But wishes sometimes grow wishes of their own. The Fate Mountains were lonely, each one sitting in its own quarter of the world, and so the mountains wished for company. Soon enough, the mountains flourished with life. Spiders began to spin magical Threads of Fate, and as these burst from the mountaintops, people were born.*'

As if hearing her words, a Fate Thread leapt on to Ember's shoulder, whizzed around her neck, and then jumped off again, rushing between the shelves.

'*Time was pleased,*' continued Ember. '*With people roaming the world, there was now a reason for keeping track of the days, and she had her four mountains to look after the future. And so it was for many years.*

'*Then, many thousands of years later, human explorers found the mountains and the desert, along with other magical landscapes around the world.*

'*As all explorers did, they mapped their findings.*'

Mapped. Ember felt a surge of excitement. She continued reading.

'*But soon, the explorers realised the power of the mountains. They realised that unscrupulous people* could manipulate the mountains and therefore the people below. So the explorers gave their maps to the mountains themselves, to keep safe. That way no one could discover and control them.'

'Those explorers must have been the first members of S.E.C.R.E.T.,' said Falcon.

'But the explorers decided to build in a way to find the maps, in case they were ever lost or stolen,' Ember carried on. 'They made it so that each map would point to one of the others: Never to Ever, Ever to Sometimes, Sometimes to When, and When back to Never. But only a special device would reveal this power. The device would remain hidden in the words that were spoken, the stories that were told, the myths that were believed.

'I, the writer, promise to keep this device hidden. Just as you, the reader, must also.'

Ember looked up.

'This is the clue we've been looking for,' she said, barely believing it herself. 'The Never Map points to the missing Ever Map. All we need is . . .' She looked back to the story. 'A device.'

'But what device?' asked Falcon.

Ember picked up the Never Map and studied it. Was there anything on there that could signal a secret device? There was no pointing arrow, no sign, no compass even—

There was no compass. 'Where's the compass?' Ember wondered aloud.

Ember knew the Never Map had been kept safe in the Know-It-Hall until her friend Flint had found it and given it to Ember. He had never mentioned a compass.

Brontey voice's broke her train of thought from above. She had been watching them all along. 'I remember when the explorers put that Never Map in here, a long time ago,' she said. 'It had a funny little piece on the top; I suppose it *could* have been a compass.'

'Do you know where it might be now?' said Ember.

Brontey shook her tiny little head and began to crawl down the shelves towards them. 'Read it again, the bit about the device.'

Ember read it aloud. '*The device would remain hidden in the words that were spoken, the stories that were told, the myths that were believed.*

'*I, the writer, promise to keep this device hidden. Just as you, the reader, must also.*' She paused for a second. 'What does that mean? Is the device in a story? A word?'

'Is it in the book?' said Falcon.

'There's nothing in it,' said Ember, rifling through the remaining pages.

'Look!' said Hans. 'It makes a funny little moving picture!'

He grabbed the book from Ember and began to flick the corners of the pages. The tiny symbols on the corner of each page blended into one moving image. It was a flip-book.

'Hans, you're a genius!' Ember said, and Hans leapt into the air, bouncing around Falcon's head.

'What picture does it make?' said Falcon, squinting at the symbols.

'Music!' said Ember, flicking them again and again. 'Brontey, please, can you whistle it for us?'

The bookworm, who had reached the bottom of the shelves, stared up at her. 'Why should I?'

'Not everything you do has to be for gain,' said Falcon, surprising Ember. 'You can do something simply because it's the right thing to do.'

Hans raised his eyebrows at Ember, then they both turned to look at Brontey. With a sigh, she wriggled over to the book.

Carefully, Ember flicked the pages to create the musical score. Brontey took a deep breath, and whistled.

For a moment, nothing happened.

Then, out of the corner of her eye, Ember saw a book flapping towards them. She caught it and immediately opened the cover – where she discovered a handwritten message on the first page.

'*Dear Explorer. Be careful. The Mountains of Fate serve Time, but Time serves no one.*'

'Does everything have to be complete nonsense?' said Falcon.

'It usually is,' said Hans. 'Life's much more fun that way.'

Ember turned the page and gasped. Someone had cut into the pages underneath to make a secret compartment! Within, secured by two small hinges, was a circular piece of glass.

Holding her breath, Ember pushed each hinge open

and the contraption came loose into the palm of her hand. The glass was housed in a metal frame, but other than that it was bare; there was no arrow, nothing that showed which way was north.

But, as she held it over the map, Ember could instantly see that it was the same size as the map's wax seal, the one which showed the S.E.C.R.E.T. symbol of the Fate Mountains, outlined with the letters N, E, S, W. Carefully, she laid the glass on to the top of the waxy border, and clipped it into place.

It fitted perfectly.

She drew her hands away and waited.

'Did it work?' said Falcon.

As they all peered closer, the seal beneath the glass started to move.

The outline of the four mountain peaks, which had been pointing up towards the N, began to wobble, as did the letters around the outside.

Soon enough, the letters N, E, S, and W were moving like a ring on their own. The mountains inside were also swinging around, independently from the letters.

Ember picked up the Never Map.

'What's happening?' said Hans, bouncing up to her shoulder to get a better look as Ember turned the map this way and that.

'The N on the outside of the seal keeps pointing towards the top of Mount Never, no matter which way I turn it,' she said.

Falcon nodded. 'And Mount Never is the northern-most mountain, so it must be pointing north.'

'Which means if we head towards the E, we'll find Mount Ever because that's in the east?' asked Hans.

'That's right,' said Ember. 'So the letters work like a normal compass. But look, the outline of the mountains in the middle of the seal is turning on its own. It's pointing between the E and the S.'

'What's it pointing to?' asked Falcon.

Ember knew already. 'The Ever Map! It's like Jasper said: the map isn't *on* Mount Ever, it's somewhere else.'

'But we need more than a general direction!' said Hans.

'Maybe that could help?' said Falcon, pointing to the back of the map.

Ember turned the map over, where an inky image

was beginning to form, lines spreading from the seal in the corner, seeping through the paper. It was creating a rough outline of the world, a smaller version of the map Jasper had shown them.

And there, in the south-east of the map, nestled inside the walls of a village, were two tiny hand-lettered words. *Ever Map*.

Without any hesitation, Hans leapt up. 'OK!' he said. 'LET'S GO!'

Just then, Ember saw Florence swooping towards them, a small envelope in her mouth.

'This is for you,' Florence said, dropping the envelope in Falcon's hands. He turned away from them to open it.

'We found directions to the Ever Map,' Ember told Florence. 'With that map, we might actually be able to find the desert, and then maybe even turn back time to stop the Thread-Cutter. We might really be able to do this,' she said.

'I have no doubt in you whatsoever,' Florence said kindly.

Ember packed the book in her bag and gripped the map tightly. She looked over at Falcon, still frowning over his note.

'Falcon,' she called over to him. 'If you want to go back to get help now, you could. I bet now that we have a concrete plan, they won't stop us.'

Ember was thinking that if Falcon went back now, she and Hans could slip away before he returned, and, without the map, no one would be able track them down. The journey would be much easier without Falcon questioning her every choice.

'It's fine,' said Falcon, looking at the watch Jasper had given him. 'I've decided you're right and we should carry on.'

'Why?' asked Ember, surprised. 'Wait – what did you tell Haywood? You didn't tell him—'

'No,' said Falcon firmly. 'But he knows I'm safe now. That's enough. Anyway, I could be helpful. I've travelled a lot with Haywood and it's always better to have an extra person on your team, right?'

'OK,' she said, still bewildered by his change of heart. 'Let's go, then.'

They looked at the back of the Never Map and at the words *Ever Map* in the south-east. Ember placed her tunnel ticket beside the map, trying to determine

144

which of S.E.C.R.E.T.'s tunnels would lead them closest to their destination.

'It looks like this stop here is the closest one to where the Ever Map is,' she said, tapping the holographic network. 'Hollowmere. We need to go through these three tunnels to get there. The first takes us to the Tremoring Tropics, the second to the Emocean, and then the last to Hollowmere itself.'

Florence took a step backwards. 'I'll wait here and keep an eye on the mountain,' she said. 'We don't want any more threads being cut while you're gone.'

'Right then,' said Falcon, checking the watch again. 'The rest of us had better hurry. We've got four and a half hours left. Ready?' Hans looked as though he might explode with excitement.

Were they ready to visit new magical realms?

'Always,' said Ember.

11

Holding her N.O.S.E. out in front of her, Ember led them back through the forest on the edge of Everspring, deeper into the woodlands, where frost had settled in the trees, cobwebs crystallised by the cold. Despite the early afternoon sun shining bright overhead, the cold bit into Ember's fingertips. With every step, the light on her ticket flashed faster and faster, showing them the way. Falcon followed, still excitedly studying his watch as they walked, while Hans shivered inside Ember's jacket.

'You're quiet,' said Ember. Hans had barely said a word since they left Mount Never.

'I was thinking,' Hans said. 'Isn't it a bit strange that Ms Daylands didn't want to do anything?'

'What do you mean?' asked Ember in surprise.

Hans shrugged. 'She was talking but she wasn't doing anything. We're the ones trying to fix everything again.'

'I guess,' said Ember. It *had* been frustrating to see Ms Daylands not act, especially since she knew about the legends of the landscapes. But Ember hadn't thought it was strange. 'I think people deal with scary situations in different ways.'

'I hope our way is the right way this time,' said Hans quietly.

Ember didn't know what to say. She had been doubting herself too. Last time she had made a decision this big, it had ended . . . well, in making things very complicated indeed. Now, every decision felt more difficult.

At that moment, the light on Ember's N.O.S.E. began to flash even more furiously until a moment later it became one solid light.

'We must be close to the tunnel entrance,' she said.

Ahead was a tall tree with brown-red coloured bark and leaves the shape of teardrops.

'Is this it?' asked Falcon. He brushed the hanging leaves out of the way, revealing a small hole in the trunk of the tree, with the word *Tickets* etched above it.

'Yes!' shouted Hans, his concern disappearing as

quickly as his worries always did.

Falcon put his pass in, and almost immediately the tree spat it back out. Then, the ground at the tree roots sank away, leaving a gaping hole where Ember could see roots woven back and forth, forming a set of steps.

'I'll go first,' said Falcon, starting down the steps. 'I'll see you down there.'

Hans followed, grinning and apparently feeling better already. Ember couldn't push aside her doubt so quickly. Were they doing the right thing? She didn't feel as though she had another choice. She couldn't lose all her memories of Hans and everything they had been through. Shaking her head to try and rattle the thought away, she got her pass checked and carefully descended the steps to where Hans and Falcon stood waiting.

Hans was bouncing up and down with excitement. 'Look! The next transport is *amaza-brillia-fabu-ling*!' he shouted.

'That's not a word, you know,' said Falcon.

'It's a made-up word, like all words are,' said Hans.

Looking at the tunnel ahead, Ember had to agree with Hans; it *was* amaza-brillia-fabu-ling.

A crystal-clear blue river began only steps away and stretched deep into the tunnel. The water looked calm and cool, glinting in the light from candles lining the walls. And there, floating on top, was their transport.

A boat.

Despite Ember's lingering fear of the water, she couldn't help but marvel at its design. It had been carved from the trunk of a large tree, hollowed out to make seats for up to six people, one in front of another. Then, Ember noticed that there were no oars.

She swallowed. She might have overcome her fear of water for the most part, but the idea of a log boat without oars still made her nervous.

'You can sit with me,' said Hans kindly, as if reading her mind.

Ember nodded and put a smile on. She didn't want to look scared in front of Falcon.

The three of them climbed into the log, Falcon at the front, and Ember and Hans behind.

'How does it work?' asked Ember. But no sooner had she finished speaking, than the log boat began to move forwards. Soon enough they were whizzing along, the river splashing up at them from beneath. Ember clung to the seat in front of her, her eyes closed as Hans squealed with excitement.

After a few minutes, Ember managed to open her eyes and gasped as she took in what was happening.

The river must have been on a track like the mud in the tunnel of baskets, but this track wove its way between the surface and underground, dipping and diving between the two like a dolphin. One minute, they were skating along the earth, then ducking back underground, coming up and going back under, the river pulling them along.

Each time they came above ground, Ember caught a glimpse of the world beyond Everspring.

It was everything she had ever dreamt of. Wild meadows filled with flowers; cities in the distance, their buildings merging into one another to create silhouettes that punctured the clouds above. The sun shone overhead, its light glowing over the fields and bouncing off the water around them. Ember had known there was more of the world, but she could never have pictured such wide, open spaces, and so much sky! Everspring, and even the colossal Mount Never,

suddenly felt minuscule as their boat rushed by lakes, volcanoes, coastlines: things she had never seen before in real life.

There is so much world to explore, thought Ember excitedly.

As they travelled, Ember noticed that the boat never passed inside a city; they always ducked below ground before reaching one. She supposed someone might notice them and wonder what a log boat was doing rushing by, carrying two children and a clock hand. She grinned; the secrecy of it all amazed her. People thought their rivers were just rivers, but really, they were secret networks! It was fantastic.

The log boat dipped underground again, taking them into the dark for a while, then back up into the glowing sunshine. Falcon looked back and beamed at her. For a second, he dropped the cool act and began to laugh.

The water sprayed up at them as they turned a corner, racing along the stream, and finally, the log slowed down a little.

Ahead, the river seemed to disappear into a dense rainforest. Ember could feel the moisture in the air, hanging around her. It was much hotter here, and her jacket stuck to her skin. As they reached the trees, they ducked through a curtain of leaves and vines, and entered the thick of a rainforest.

Canopies of leaves overhead let in puddles of sunlight here and there. Beneath, moss clung to trunks, vines wrapped around one another and wound through the trees like snakes, and the whole place was alive with sounds.

'Wow,' whispered Hans.

The boat was moving even more slowly now. Along the side of the river, a family of orange froghoppers leapt over one another as they travelled through the jungle. Further along, a black bird with a curved rainbow beak looked down on them and let out a loud *caw*, while a pair of polka-dot-tailed lemurs hung from the branches, playing.

Everywhere Ember turned, a different animal seemed to be looking down at them, curious about the three visitors.

Juniper would love it here, thought Ember with a smile, and she felt a guilty tug on her heart. One day, she'd take Juniper here, when the danger was past.

The river came to an end, and they climbed out of the log boat on to the surprisingly squishy floor of the rainforest. They had made it to the Tremoring Tropics.

'Where now?' asked Falcon.

Ember pulled out the Never Map and her N.O.S.E. and took another look. They were closer to the south-east, but still quite far from where the words *Ever Map* were written.

'Next, we need to take a tunnel to the Emocean. From there, it's only one more tunnel to Hollowmere,' she said, pushing the tunnel entrance on her ticket. Immediately, the light on the end began to blink. Slowly, she turned around in a circle until it was clear where the N.O.S.E. was directing them.

'The next tunnel should be this way,' said Ember. 'Let's go.'

They began walking, and Ember couldn't stop looking at the sights around her. There were plants that shook their leaves in greeting as Ember walked by, and a snake with a rattle that sounded like a windchime.

'This is better than that big library, huh?' Falcon said, seeing her face.

Ember grinned at him. *Maybe Falcon isn't so bad*, she thought.

But at her smile, he suddenly frowned and began walking faster. 'Come on, hurry up,' he said gruffly.

Ember looked at Hans, wide-eyed and confused. Hans shrugged back. 'Maybe he stepped on a fun-zapping-wasp?' he whispered.

Ember couldn't work Falcon out at all. One minute he was nice, the next completely rude. He had flipped from trying to persuade them to go back to Haywood, to telling *them* to hurry up. *It must be difficult trying to be something different every two minutes*, she thought.

'How long do we have left, Falcon?' asked Hans.

'About four hours,' he called back to them. 'But the hand is moving much quicker in here than it did in Everspring . . .' He trailed off. 'What's that?' he said.

Ember could hear it too. A new noise was building around them. To begin with, it sounded like muffled, shrieking nonsense, but, slowly, Ember could make out one voice, shouting above the rest.

With a worried look at Falcon, she put her finger to her mouth in a 'be quiet' movement, then protectively scooped Hans up. They walked on more carefully now, still following the light of Ember's N.O.S.E., past a cluster of plants that shrank in on themselves as they passed, and through a grove of trees with holey leaves. The yelling grew louder and louder, until they reached the edge of a clearing. They came to a halt and peeked through the leaves, searching for the source of the voice.

At the entrance to the clearing, on an extremely tall chair made from a tree trunk, sat a large monkey wearing a wide-brimmed hat.

And in the clearing was chaos.

On the ground there were glowing, luminescent vines, arranged into shapes. As Ember studied them, she realised it was a map of the world, the same as the one they'd seen back at S.E.C.R.E.T., but made of vines rather than ink. Hanging above the clearing was an elaborate contraption, like a conveyor belt, with seven different claws hanging from it.

Swinging between trees, gathering round the vine-map, and climbing on top of the motionless conveyor belt, was a squabble of monkeys. They were not much bigger than Hans, and each one was mostly covered with soft black fur, but they had long white tails and white bellies. Ember could hardly keep track of them as they crossed the belt, leapt into the trees, rushed off into the jungle and then returned. Every single one was frantically scurrying round, as the monkey in the tall chair shouted instructions to them.

'Come on, team! We haven't got all day!' the leader-monkey called, clapping his hands together. 'Oh this is not good, not good at all,' he cried.

'What is going *on*?' whispered Ember, perplexed.

As far as she could tell, they were in a *huge* panic. The question was – why?

12

All of a sudden, as Ember watched, the conveyor belt above the world map jerked forwards, then stopped, juddered, and reversed back. There was a tall, metal machine to one side, which seemed to be powering the belt, and it let out a long moan as the belt gave another judder. Ember saw that beside the machine there was a table full of strange objects such as brown bags, fabric pouches, and a collection of jars. A monkey kept piling more and more on top.

'Come on, team! Keep moving, we can do it!' the largest monkey called out. From high up on his chair, he continued to shout orders, clearly desperate to keep things running smoothly. Hanging down below, swishing in front of them, was his tail—

Ember gasped. The end of his tail was the strangest of shapes – it bulged into a circle with a small hole in it, before stretching out into a long shape with distinct grooves and short prongs, like a . . .

'Look!' she whispered to Hans and Falcon. 'It's a key!'

These weren't monkeys, they were mon-keys!

'Alto!' the mon-key leader said. 'Get your head out of the clouds and drop them over section seven-c!'

A tiny mon-key, with a tiny key tail, climbed across the conveyor belt, urgently pushing others out of the way. In his hands, Ember saw a grey puff of what looked like smoke, but with a soft silver lining.

A rain cloud! Ember realised.

With a worried look on his face, the mon-key dropped it over the map. It came to a halt a few inches above the map, trembled, and then released a shower below before dissolving into the air.

'That was quadrant *six*-c!' shouted the boss mon-key. 'Oh come on, team, we have to do better than this. With the machine broken it's up to us!'

Of course, realised Ember. *The conveyer belt is broken; without it the mon-keys are having to work double time to keep up with the changing weather.*

No wonder they seemed so stressed.

A mon-key came sprinting on two legs through the forest to the clearing. 'Boss!' she screamed. 'Boss! I've lost the eye of the hurricane! I've only got hurr and cane now! I've got a *hurrcane*!'

'It'll have to do,' shouted the boss. 'Cirrus, take the hurrcane from Strato and drop it over three-b please. Quickly now!'

Just then, Ember spotted a strange thing on the ground in front of them. It looked like a disc covered in dust. The middle was still, but the dust at the edge was whizzing around the outside. She picked it up, very carefully, and realised what it was.

After a moment's deliberation, she stepped forwards.

'Excuse me!' she called. 'I think I found the "i" of the hurricane.'

Every single mon-key stopped in its tracks, and turned to look at her.

A stillness fell over the forest, until . . .

'Don't just stand there, Cirrus! Turn that hurrcane into a hurricane!' shouted the leader.

Cirrus leapt down from the belt, nimbly crawled around the outside of the map, and grabbed the 'i' from Ember. Within moments, he was back on the top of the map, tipping the complete hurricane over it.

The boss mon-key looked down at Ember for a moment, then turned back to the book in his arms. 'Right-o, team. We've got a break in the weather for the moment. I'd say it's enough time for someone to get under the weather and see what's going on with the machine.'

The mon-keys all leapt from their positions to the contraption, and started to study it, clearly desperately trying to find out what was wrong.

'You there,' said the boss mon-key to Ember. 'Who are you? Did Topaz send you?

Ember shook her head. 'Topaz?' she asked.

'Topaz Blackthorne?' he said. 'The agent assigned to our landscape.'

'Oh, no,' said Ember. 'I'm Ember, this is Hans, and that's Falcon. We're with S.E.C.R.E.T. Sort of.'

'Right,' he said, and glanced back to his team at the map, calling out to them again. 'Can we get a rain check please? We've got a downpour coming and I don't want the machine raining cats and dogs like last time, is that clear?'

He turned back to Ember. 'I'm Nimbo and I'm afraid you've caught us on a bad day. Machine's

161

broken so we're running the weather ourselves. Usually, our main job is unlocking the trees to harvest the weather from the rainforest, then we use this machine to make sure it goes to exactly the right place. Now that it's broken, we're doing the deliveries ourselves.'

'Look!' said Hans, nudging Ember and pointing up to a treetop ahead of them. There, a small mon-key was pushing its tail into a hole in the tree. Carefully, it turned it, and the bark opened like a door. The mon-key reached in and pulled out what appeared to be two tiny bow-ties . . . which looked like they were made of water.

'Double rainbow!' said Nimbo. 'Don't see those every day.'

All of a sudden, another mon-key came swinging through the trees and straight towards Nimbo, carrying a teapot in one hand, a teacup in another.

'Sir!' they said. 'I've got a storm in a teacup and another one brewing!'

Nimbo sighed and rubbed his head. 'Right, give me the teacup – it'll last a while before going off – and you'll have to use that pot for the downpour.' He looked over to Cirrus, Strato and the rest of the team. 'Places, everyone, we're putting a downpour over section eighteen-b.'

Ember watched as the mon-keys once again delivered the weather. They were slightly more accurate this time, with Nimbo muttering under his breath that eighteen-c wasn't too bad.

'Can someone get me some lightning in a bottle, please?' he called. 'And for goodness' sake, let's not strike the same place *again*. The people down there get funny about that.'

Ember stepped forwards. 'Mind if I take a look at your machine?' she asked. 'I might be able to help.'

Falcon narrowed his eyes. 'Ember, we've got to get a move on! We don't have time for this.'

But Nimbo had already hopped down from his log-chair. 'Sure, take a look. Topaz was meant to be on his way to help. But if you're with S.E.C.R.E.T., then I suppose you could do the job. After all, S.E.C.R.E.T. are supposed to have the world's finest inventors. We mon-keys are meteorologists, not mechanics. We haven't even worked out how to open it up!'

'We can't leave them like this,' Ember said to Falcon. 'Not if we can help.'

Hans hopped out of Ember's jacket. 'Yeah, and we're the best inventors, so we'll be super-duper-fast.'

The pair of them hurried over to the table, where mon-keys were continuing to drop off different weathers – storms brewed in teapots, jacket pockets full of sunshine, even a bag of wind, which made Hans giggle a little.

The machine looked fairly straightforward to Ember; it seemed to be a typical conveyor belt with claws. The claw was supposed to open, a mon-key would give it the weather, input the destination on the keypad, and then the machine would move it along and drop it at the right place.

But something clearly wasn't working. Opening her bag, Ember took out her toolkit and chose her favourite screwdriver. With a careful twist, she popped open a panel on the machine's side. There, she found the cogs that turned the machine's belt. Each one fitted perfectly on to the next, and moving the first should have led to the second moving, and then the third and so on, until together they moved the belt. But it seemed there had been a problem; the cogs weren't turning at all. Ember leant in, pushing her head inside so she could get a better look, and immediately spotted the issue.

Pulling her head out, she frowned and said to Nimbo, 'Somehow, one of the cogs has frozen over! It's covered in ice and won't turn!'

Nimbo rolled his eyes and nodded. 'We had a blizzard last week. Those things can really run wild, you know?'

Run wild? Ember shook her head, and Falcon and Hans both looked as confused as she felt.

'You know? Blizzards? Four legs, ice-cold, bright blue?' asked Nimbo.

'Do you mean . . . lizards?' asked Falcon.

'No, you fool, *blizzards*. The lizard's colder-blooded relative,' explained Nimbo.

'Well, however it happened,' Ember said, 'I think I can fix it.' She turned to Hans. 'Can you get me a flat-headed screwdriver, please?'

He immediately obliged.

As Ember started to work, gently chipping the ice off from around the cog with the tip of the screwdriver, she heard Hans chattering away to Nimbo.

'Nimbo, are all of your keys the same?' he asked.

'No, we're all unique,' said Nimbo. 'It's what makes us special.'

'But all of you have *some* sort of key,' said Hans thoughtfully. 'You still belong together.'

'Of course. We're a family,' said Nimbo.

'Did you always have each other?' asked Hans.

'Mon-keys have been in these tropics for centuries,' said Nimbo. 'We've never *not* had one another.'

Ember, working inside the machine, felt her eyes threaten tears. She had seen how disappointed Hans had been in S.E.C.R.E.T. on finding out there was no one else like him. He was clearly still thinking about family and fitting in. She wished he could see that he already fitted in. He fitted in with *her*.

Once she had broken off all the ice, she blinked back her tears and turned to Nimbo.

'That should do it,' she said.

'Why don't you test it?' said Nimbo. 'Let's have a pocket of sunshine over thirteen-b.'

'Really?' squealed Hans, suddenly bouncing with glee again.

Ember laughed, reached over to the table and grabbed one of the pockets, its warm glow escaping from the top. She passed it to Hans, who held it under one of the claws. The claw immediately grabbed it, and Ember punched in the destination into the keypad.

The claw glided across the machine to the correct section and dropped the warm glow right over thirteen-b – which Ember suddenly realised was Everspring.

'YES!' shouted Hans. 'Inventing wonder-duo Hans and Ember strike again!'

Ember was always grateful for how quickly Hans seemed to be able to shake off a spell of sadness.

'Wonderful!' said Nimbo. 'Everyone, let's work the weather double time to catch up!'

The mon-keys around them sprang into action, some of them cheering and patting Ember on the head as they swung by.

'And to say thank you, take this,' Nimbo said, handing her the storm in a teacup. It was a beautiful white cup with a cloud pattern around the outside. Within it, tiny grey clouds were rumbling and growing. 'It usually keeps for a day or so. Just pull the handle on the teacup to release the storm.'

'Are you sure?' Ember asked, beyond excited.

'Of course,' said Nimbo. He thanked her once more, and then scurried back to his chair, ready to give orders again.

Falcon nudged her and held up his N.O.S.E., which was blinking slowly. 'Come on,' he said. 'We've still got a map to find, and it's a long way away yet.'

Ember carefully put the storm in her bag, wondering when she might ever have the chance to use something like *that*, and they set off to find the next tunnel.

13

It took them a few wrong turns but eventually Ember, Falcon and Hans found the entrance to their next tunnel hidden behind an enormous, hungry-looking plant with leaves that looked suspiciously like a mouth. Avoiding its open petal-jaws, they had their tickets checked by the little slot, then descended a set of steps into the tunnel's entrance.

Ember thought she was used to expecting the unexpected, but the tunnel's design still caught her by surprise. It was dark, as usual, but there was no sign of any transport. Instead, there was a metallic footpath with wooden barriers either side, a silver handrail topping each one. She was about to open her mouth to worry aloud how long it might take them to walk to the Emocean, but she stopped herself. Things were *never* as they seemed.

She stepped on to the footpath, and Falcon and Hans followed.

'Maybe we should hold on to the rail,' she said. 'We don't know what—'

Even as she spoke, the walkway sprang to life, pulling them forwards. Slowly, it gathered speed, and Ember gripped the rail. Hans grabbed her leg as the walkway whizzed them forwards.

The tunnel grew brighter and brighter until, all of a sudden, the dirt around them disappeared, replaced by incredible glass walls, arching all the way overhead. Ember gasped, while Hans collapsed on to his back, flat on the speedy walkway.

'We're . . .' Hans began, 'we're . . .'

'*Inside* the ocean!' squealed Ember.

It was like they were swimming with the sea creatures, zooming along on the ocean floor. There were incredible animals everywhere Ember looked. It was as though the pages of her schoolbooks had come to life. Flying fish zoomed past them, their wings flapping in the water. Along the seabed, a clutter of crabs warded off a group of angry hufferpufferfish. Two swordfish were having a fencing match while seahorses cheered, their hooves pounding the floor. Ember could barely catch a glimpse of every species

they saw – until, suddenly, it grew dark.

Looking up, she watched in wonder as an enormous whale passed overhead, its underbelly so close that Ember could see the bumpy texture of its skin.

'*This* is the Emocean?' she asked, dazed.

'It's not what I'd imagined either,' said Falcon, gazing through the glass in amazement.

Gradually, the ocean became emptier, fewer fish flew past them, and the vibrant colours were swapped

for the constant blue of the sea water. Ember could sense they were far out in the depths of the ocean now; the world above felt much further away.

Eventually, the walkway began to slow.

Ember, who was still looking out through the glass, noticed a strange colour appear in the water. It was a marbled purple, swirling through the ocean like oil. A moment later Ember spotted another swirl of colour ahead, this one bright orange and much larger.

Then, all around them, a colourful reef began to form, plants and coral and rocks of all shapes and sizes, knobbly and thin, large and holey. Meanwhile, more and more inky swirls floated past.

The walkway slowed further until Ember saw their tunnel coming to an end in an open space, like an enormous underwater igloo. And there, wearing a pale blue dress that skimmed the floor as she walked forward, was a graceful woman with long, straight black hair and a striking, angular face.

'You must be Ember, Falcon, and lovely little Hans,' she said, as the walkway came to a stop in front of her. 'It's such a pleasure to meet you!'

They stepped off the walkway, and already Hans had begun to bounce around the space.

'You know who we are?' asked Ember cautiously.

'Of course,' said the woman. 'I'm May Ripple, agent assigned to the Emocean. The whole of S.E.C.R.E.T. is buzzing about you and your mission to find the desert.'

'Really?' said Ember. She hadn't thought anyone else in S.E.C.R.E.T. would have known about her, but she did remember Anise mentioning May. 'We've found the location of the Ever Map. We're on our way there now.'

'That's brilliant,' said May encouragingly.

Falcon showed Ember his watch. 'We need to hurry. We've only got just over two hours left,' he explained. 'At least the hand is moving more slowly here.'

'Still, we'd better go,' said Ember.

'Absolutely,' said May. 'The other tunnel entrances are all that way,' she said, gesturing to the far side of the room.

Ember tried to take in as much as possible as they crossed the small glass building. The coral reef around them was beautiful, fabulous rocks and organisms all clustered together like a miniature city. Every so often, one would release the strange oil-marble liquid, which would swirl around, and then be carried off by the current.

At one end of the room, there were a few armchairs – all higgledy-piggledy and mismatched – and two wide, short shelves, curved to fit the glass walls. On the first shelf was a collection of identical thermometers; each stood in its own brass frame and was filled with a different coloured liquid. The second shelf was home to a host of empty bottles.

'Ready, Ember?' said Falcon. He gestured to three trapdoors on the floor. 'The entrance for the tunnel to Hollowmere must be one of these.'

'Wait, I have a joke!' said Hans with a stifled laugh. 'Do you know why the ocean blushed?'

'Why?' said Ember with a wry smile, already knowing the answer.

Hans held back a giggle. 'Because the sea weed!' he cried. 'Seaweed!'

Before Ember could even smile, Falcon erupted with laughter, so forceful that he doubled over. Ember and Hans looked at each other, wide-eyed; Falcon hadn't laughed once yet, so hearing him break into giggles at Hans' silly joke was unbelievable! But soon enough, his laughter infected Hans and Ember, and they were all howling uncontrollably.

'Come on, Hans,' said Ember, still giggling. 'Unless you want me to forget all about—'

'No, no, no!' May shouted from behind them.

Their laughter stopped as quickly as it had begun. Ember and Falcon exchanged a worried look and hurried back over to May, whose pale skin had turned grey with fear.

'We've got too much envy, far too much!' she muttered, dashing over to the thermometer shelf.

Hans leapt up against the glass wall. 'That coral is going a little bit woopy-doo isn't it?'

A spongey plant on the other side of the glass was squeezing in and out as though it was breathing heavily, angrily. Suddenly, it erupted, lime-green inky liquid bursting out and covering the other plants around it. It kept going, more and more seeping out until everything was covered in green.

'This is happening more and more frequently,' May said, her voice worried. 'There's far too much going out at once!'

The green swirl built and built until it was like an enormous cloud, surrounding the entire building, and then, finally, it shot to the top of the water and their view was clear again.

'It's gone,' said May. 'Nothing I can do now.' She sounded on the verge of tears.

'Did that feeling belong to a person?' asked Hans.

'It will do soon, I'm afraid,' May said, with a sniff.

'Let me try to explain. Hans, when you told your joke before, you made Ember and Falcon laugh. Well, that happiness didn't spark from nothing; it started here in the Emocean. The happiness would have lapped up on shore one day, spread through someone at the beach, who might have passed it on to someone else, and on and on until eventually, it reached you, and you chose to pass it on to Ember and Falcon.'

'Wow,' said Hans, enthralled.

May smiled and continued. 'Unfortunately, sometimes people don't pass happiness on and it stays inside them, unused. So, the Emocean needs to send out more and more. It can do that for a while, but not for ever. Emotions are natural resources within reefs, and once a reef has sent out all its resources, it dries up. Have a look at the Reef of Kindness over here, for example.'

She led them across the room and pointed at a patch of coral that was stark white. It had no colour left at all.

May looked at it sadly. 'The Emocean has been spreading kindness for years, trying to counter the lack of it in some people. But eventually it ran out. Now the only way kindness can reproduce is if we spread it ourselves. Eventually, if there's enough of it, that kindness might end up back in the Emocean, ready to be sent out again.'

Ember nodded. It was confusing, but she thought she was beginning to understand.

'It's a little bit like a forest,' she suggested. 'A healthy forest can grow new trees, and we can even plant our own. But if we chop them down again and again, eventually the forest will find it really hard to grow any new ones by itself?'

'Exactly!' said May. 'Although, *I'm* still hoping for a miracle. You see, there is a legend that in very, *very* rare cases, a truly remarkable action could trigger an emotion being made here, in the Emocean, whether the reef had used up all its resources or not!' continued May. 'Imagine that! An act so kind it would regenerate this whole reef! Sadly, we've never seen that happen.'

She turned back to the reef. 'So now, when there's a need for a certain emotion, like happiness or kindness, but the Emocean doesn't have any left, its only option is to send out another emotion in its place. Like envy, for example.' She held up a thermometer filled with the

179

same green liquid they had just seen in the ocean. Scratched into the rounded part at the bottom was the word *Envy*. 'These devices measure emotion levels in the world. Look, now envy levels are through the roof!'

Falcon looked out at the Emocean. 'What do you do then?' he said. 'Surely S.E.C.R.E.T. has some . . . invention or something to balance the emotions?'

May's eyes lit up. 'Oh yes, it's one of my own actually.' She hurried over to the shelf, where she grabbed a long tube that had a funny pump on one end. In her other hand, she was holding a packet of thin needles.

'What is *that*?' asked Hans.

'It's an emotion-extractor,' said May. 'It's a little bit cheeky, but I've found that some people have enormous stores full of unused emotions. For example, I'm not scared of much, so there's plenty of fear in me that simply doesn't get used. Other people absorb kindness faster than they pass it on.'

'So you take their extra emotions?' asked Ember, intrigued by the idea.

'I always leave enough for them to use when they

need it,' said May, looking at them rather pleadingly. 'I know it's a bit scary, but it helps so many people. If you've got enough, why not give? Is it something . . . you might consider?'

'Absolutely!' said Hans. 'Take some from me!'

May's face fell slightly. 'I'm so sorry, Hans. I don't think I have any needles for metal skin.'

'Oh. OK,' Hans said, and he returned to Ember, kicking the floor as he went.

'But I promise, I'll make one soon,' May said gently. 'No one should be left out of offering kindness.'

May turned to Ember and Falcon, who looked at one another awkwardly. Ember certainly didn't like the idea of having a needle stuck in her, but if it helped other people . . .

'OK,' she said. 'You can do me. But we don't have much time.'

'I'll be quick as a fox,' said May. 'Let's get started!'

She grabbed a few empty bottles from the shelf, ushered Ember to a pink, tattered armchair, and within moments had attached the needle to the tube, and carefully placed it into Ember's arm, under the skin.

'It's a special kindness needle,' she said. 'It isolates

that emotion only. Now, let's see if you have any going spare.'

Soon enough, a gold, ink-like liquid trickled from the tube into a bottle next to Ember. 'I didn't think kindness was an emotion,' said Ember thoughtfully.

'Of course it is! You can feel kind some days and selfish others, can't you? Oh wow,' said May in amazement, looking at the kindness being extracted from Ember. 'See that bronze-like element in it? That means it's not pure kindness from the Emocean. It shows that you've had a lot of kindness passed on to you.'

That was true, for sure. Her own father had died saving her. Juniper was always doing kind things for her. And of course she had Hans as a best friend.

But within seconds, the tube trickled dry. 'Hmm,' said May. 'It looks as though you must have done something quite kind recently. You've don't have many reserves.'

'She did,' said Hans. 'She fixed the machine in the Tremoring Tropics!'

May smiled. 'Wonderful! You see, kindness sparks kindness. Your kind act will inspire someone else to act kindly, and that act will inspire another, and so on. Soon enough, someone will do a kind thing for you, and your reserves will fill right back up!' She turned to Falcon. 'How about you then, Falcon?'

Falcon nodded, but his expression was odd. Almost scared.

As soon as the needle was inserted, golden liquid started to flow into the tube, gushing out in huge quantities. 'Wow!' said May. 'What an awful lot of kindness you have to spare,' she said, grabbing a third bottle.

'I do nice things too though,' he said defensively. 'All the time.'

'Maybe you're doing them for a different reason than kindness. Sometimes, we do them so people will accept us, or show us affection, rather than simply to be kind.'

Falcon looked down at his hands.

'The important thing is to keep doing good, no matter what,' said May, and she squeezed his hand. 'And let me tell you something, this kindness is going to help so many people!'

She released the needle from Falcon, whose golden

kindness trickled down on to his dark copper skin, and hurried with the bottles over to the glass directly in front of the white section of reef. Crouching down, she opened a small panel on the floor to reveal a funnel. Little by little, she tipped Ember and Falcon's kindness into the funnel, and then closed the panel.

Within moments, the coral reef began to change colour, glowing a bright gold, and a second later it was squirting droplets from an opening in its top.

'Perfect!' said May. 'Thank you so much, especially you, Falcon. Let me see, I'm sure there's something here I can give you as a thank you.'

'You don't need to—'

'Just a moment,' said May, and she began rummaging amongst the bottles on the shelf. Finally, she pulled one free – a small, cork-stoppered glass bottle. 'That should do. Here you go,' she said, handing him the bottle.

'A little bout of bravery. For when you really need it,' said May.

Falcon blushed and stammered a thank you, pushing it into his pocket before Ember could take a proper look.

'Now, which tunnel do you need?' asked May, standing over the three trapdoors.

'We're going to Hollowmere,' said Ember.

'This one then,' said May, and held open the middle door. The three of them walked down the steps and May closed the door above. 'See you soon!' she called.

'I like her,' said Hans, grinning. 'She made Falcon go all red, and *that* was amazing.'

The three of them burst into laughter again, and Ember thought she might finally be getting used to having Falcon around.

14

This tunnel's transport turned out to be an incredibly fast mine-cart. It brought them out in a grassy field. Behind them was a forest, its ground scattered with autumn leaves, while ahead, Ember could see the walls of a city in the distance. Despite the bright sun overhead, the chilly air bit at her nose.

She pulled the map out of her bag and turned it over. There were the inky words *Ever Map*, printed inside the city walls. Glancing up, she could see those very walls, and the city that grew from within like an enormous plant in a pot.

'Two hours left,' said Falcon.

'At least time will stick to the rules here,' Ember muttered, for once grateful to not be in a magical landscape, but in the normal world where time ticked as it should. Giving them a time limit was absolutely *pointless* when they had to go through magical landscapes. They were losing hours all over the place.

'Falcon, what's Overwood like?' Hans asked as they hurried towards the city.

'I don't know,' he said. 'That's Haywood's village, not mine. I don't have one any more.'

'What do you mean? How can you not have a village?' asked Ember. 'Or, come to think of it, a surname?'

He shrugged and walked faster.

'And what do you mean, you don't have a village *any more*. Did you used to have one?'

Falcon stopped suddenly and turned around. 'I used to. But I don't any more. OK?' He seemed to spit the words out, and then stomped off ahead.

Ember frowned, looking after him. She felt a pang of sympathy for him, despite his rudeness. It must be *tiring* being on the edge of anger all the time.

'Don't worry, Ember,' whispered Hans. 'Once he understands that we're his friends, he'll feel better and tell us everything!'

As they neared the city walls, Ember could make out the two tall iron gates at the front. She tried to take everything in – the smoke overhead, the buildings emerging from the top of the walls, the incredible size of the open iron gates. It all seemed very different from Everspring. But then, that was hardly surprising now she knew Everspring was a tiny dot on an enormous world.

It looked as though there was a market outside the city. But as she got closer, Ember realised it was a collection of huts, caravans and houses made from the most ingenious materials – leaves, wooden strips, iron sheets, old tents and pieces of clothing. The first one, a wooden house on four large wheels, had been painted with intricate floral patterns.

'It's the girl!' shouted a voice from within one of the homes. 'It's Ember Shadows!'

Immediately, whispers erupted around the camp-like settlement. The doors burst open, and people ran into their path. They were all dressed in bright colours, with floral embroidery bordering the edge of capes, shawls, and thick jackets.

'What's going on?' asked Ember. They had no choice but to go through the camp to get to the city, but she suddenly felt uncomfortable. These people knew her, and there could only be one reason why.

Stepping out of a beautiful white yurt, one woman

broke through the crowd, her snowy hair tumbling all the way down to her ankles.

'Ember Shadows!' she said, smiling. She wore a cloak, similar to Ms Daylands' but in a dark purple, with embroidered tulips trimming the edges. 'We're so pleased to see you!'

'You are? What about me?' asked Hans.

'Of course you as well, Hans! What would Ember be without her helper?' said the woman, crouching down and kissing Hans on the top of his pointed head.

Hans leapt into the air and did loop-the-loops around them. Falcon, on the other hand, seemed to be hiding behind Ember, awkwardly avoiding the woman's gaze.

'It's nice to meet you,' said Ember warily, though the woman hadn't actually introduced herself. 'But we're actually in a bit of a hurry.'

'Of course. We just wanted to say thank you.'

'Thank you?'

'For getting rid of the cards,' said the woman.

'Oh . . . I—'

'Everyone in our community was banished from their own village because of the Fate Cards,' the woman began. 'We were all cast aside because our cards said we would do terrible things in the future. But you gave us a second chance at life. Once you rewrote the cards, we realised we could do anything! We travelled here to start over.'

Ember looked around. 'I— I don't know what to say.'

'No need to say anything.' The woman smiled kindly. 'My name is Freesia. My fate said I would steal from my neighbours. Sadly, when I was cast out of my village, it became truth – it was the only way I could survive. It made me believe my Fate Card must be true. But thanks to you, I can live a different life now. We all can.'

'Why don't you live inside the city?' Hans asked.

Freesia raised her eyebrows. '*That* is a good question,' she said. 'We thought it would be better to start afresh somewhere people had never had Fate Cards. That's why we came here, to the south-east. But I'm afraid even here, some people don't want to welcome us into their towns with open arms. We can come and go in the day but *living* in the city is apparently out of the question. We seem to have a . . . reputation.'

'But that's ridiculous,' said Ember, frustration beginning to boil. 'The Fate Cards showed *one* future you might have had. The machine and your belief in the cards made it come true; but it's not the only way your life could go!'

Freesia held up her hand. 'I know. You're not the only one who is angry about it.'

'Yeah,' agreed Hans. 'I'm angry too.'

'You and many others, Hans,' whispered Freesia, suddenly intense. 'Lots of the banished feel as though something was taken from them long ago – the chance for a happy life. Back then, we all believed it was our divine fate. But now we know it was only a woman and a machine, it's difficult. Many want . . . revenge.'

Moira had taken so much, Ember thought. There were people whose lives had been ruined because of the cards . . . and people whose lives had been ruined because of the *end* of the cards.

She felt Falcon nudge her back, reminding her of their deadline.

'I'm glad removing the cards has given you freedom. We really do have to get going though – it's urgent,' said Ember.

'Of course,' Freesia said, and stepped aside. Ember and Hans waved and began to walk on, but Falcon rushed past and sprinted up the path.

'Don't you *want* to get the map in time?' he called back.

Ember rolled her eyes and followed him.

Once they crossed the boundary into the city, Ember felt as though they had stepped into a dream.

The houses were tall, many storeys high, like nothing she had ever seen in Everspring. Not only that but everything, everywhere she looked, seemed to be an invention. There were small clear tubes connecting the buildings, zigzagging through the air from one house's roof to the next. And as Ember watched, she saw tiny envelopes were being carried along in them, an incredible postal system, right above her head. To her right, she saw a door surrounded by jars filled with fireflies, lighting the front steps in a warm glow. Beyond the house was a river where an enormous wheel was churning the water, powering something.

It was an inventor's city.

For the size of the city, Ember noticed the streets were strangely quiet, with only a few people strolling about, popping in and out of shops and houses, all of which were painted in misshapen blocks of black and white. None seemed to have been built quite straight either; they leaned on one another, chimneys twisted towards the sky, wonky doors facing the street and windows looking out at an angle.

It felt like a special town, where people had the freedom to create and do whatever they liked. Yet still, they let those *outside* live in a makeshift camp. Why weren't they sharing their inventions and resources?

Hans bounced next to her, his eyes locking on one thing, then another and another until he practically exploded with excitement, leaping like a firework above their heads. 'It's amazing, it's super, it's wonderful, it's—'

'Time we hurried up,' said Falcon. He looked at Ember's map, checking which direction the mountains were pointing. 'Come on!'

Ember glared at him. This was *her* quest; *she* was the one holding the Never Map, not him. But she pushed the jealousy aside. The most important thing was finding the fourth map.

Falcon led them down an alleyway between two houses that towered so close together, only a sliver of sunlight shone through.

Suddenly, Ember heard a high-pitched voice, carrying loudly through the air.

'It sounds perfect to me – everyone knowing their path in life, knowing what will happen,' it said.

Ember stopped and gestured to Falcon to wait. The voice was coming from a small glass window that had been cracked open. Ember crept towards it and peered inside.

It seemed to be some sort of city hall, and there was a meeting in progress. The room was packed, and Ember realised this must have been why the streets were so quiet. One man, in a burgundy jacket with a long tail, stood at the front, while the audience sat in rows facing him. A woman near the front was standing and had turned to face the rest of the crowd. It reminded Ember of the meeting they had held in Everspring only yesterday.

'Don't you agree?' the woman continued. 'It sounds like things would be so much easier if we knew our futures.'

'It's out of the question. Fates shouldn't be controlled like that!' shouted someone from the back. 'I'm glad *we* never got Fate Cards.'

'He's right,' said the man standing at the front as the woman sat down. 'Having your path laid out for you might sound nice, but only if you like the path you're given. These people were given terrible destinies.

Some were mere children when they received their cards, and they were banished. You must have seen them outside the city walls. They have done nothing wrong; they simply want a home, a real home.'

'We can't let 'em in here, that's for sure,' said a woman, standing to be heard. 'If their card said they'd be trouble then we can't risk it!'

'The cards showed only one person's many possible futures. If *we* had cards here, yours may very well have said something bad – it doesn't make it true. Doesn't everyone deserve a chance *not* to be trouble?' said the man at the front.

'Not my fault they had a Fateweaver, is it?'

Ember felt like shouting through the glass – it wasn't *their* fault either!

It was so complicated. Every time Ember thought she understood an argument, she learnt another one, and things were thrown into confusion again.

Maybe people *would* be better off not remembering the Fate Cards at all. Maybe S.E.C.R.E.T. was right – if they wiped everyone's memories, no one would remember the injustice, and everyone would be able to live believing they had a choice, and had always had one.

The people who had been exiled might be welcomed anywhere.

The citizens of Everspring wouldn't be panicking about having to make decisions.

The residents of Hollowmere would have no reason to suspect strangers who came to their city walls.

'Come *on*,' hissed Falcon, grabbing her elbow. 'We're running out of time.'

Ember looked back down at the map and swallowed the lump in her throat. Whatever happened with the memories, if they wanted to save the Thread-Cutter's victims, they *had* to find the Ever Map. The only way was to turn back time.

She led them right down another alleyway, then left, through the city until they reached a row of houses built against the inside of the city walls.

With each step, she pushed down her worries.

The map had led them to a tall, colourful house, with a painted purple roof. Every single building they'd seen in the city had been black and white but for this one; each splodge of paint on it was a different colour. It was a peculiar shape too; it sort of bent round to one side a little, so the roof didn't point directly up, but to the left, like the handle of a walking cane. The door was bright turquoise with an orange knocker in the centre.

'Look,' said Falcon, pointing at the map in Ember's hands. The four mountain peaks in the S.E.C.R.E.T. symbol were pointing directly towards the front door and vibrating as if they were a pin on a magnet.

They had finally arrived at the location of the fourth and final map.

15

Ember could feel her anticipation building as they looked up at the strange house.

For a moment, no one said a word. They were really here. Hans began to hop, bouncing as the tension built, until suddenly . . .

'LET'S GET IT!' he screamed, and went to bolt towards the door. Ember caught him just in time.

'We can't run into someone's house, Hans. We'll have to knock.'

The three of them stood on the colourfully painted step in front of the door. Ember had an awful memory of when they had entered the Fateweaver's home. She shuddered. At least *this* building wouldn't sway from side to side.

But what else might lie behind the door?

Slowly, she knocked twice.

From behind the door, Ember heard a scurrying noise. Then, a long, thin brass tube emerged from right above their heads. At the end was a single piece of glass that wormed its way right in front of Ember's face. It was a telescope, she realised, and it was checking who they were. It kept inching closer until it was almost touching her nose, so she stepped back, and tumbled down the step.

'Use your feet!' a voice shouted from inside.

Moments later, the door swung open to reveal a figure as equally bizarre as his home.

The man who stood at the door was holding the end of the telescope in one hand, a long wooden spoon in the other. His beard, which was as white as Mount Never's marshmallow fog, had been wrapped around his neck like a scarf. He wore a deep purple velvet shirt, buttoned beneath his beard, and black trousers.

And although he seemed full of life, Ember thought he *must* have been more than a hundred years old. Or ninety, at *least*!

He waved his spoon around in the air. 'Aren't you going to come in? No point standing out in the cold.'

He turned and walked into the house. Ember, Hans, and Falcon all took a quick glance at one another, and Hans covered his mouth, trying not to let out a nervous giggle.

This is certainly a peculiar man in a peculiar house, thought Ember.

Ember was wary about going into a stranger's home, but at least she was with Hans and Falcon. And if they didn't go in . . . they would never find the Ever Map.

Cautiously, they followed him inside to a hallway. A flight of steps led up to the floor above. Around them, doors of all sorts of shapes and sizes lined the hall, each as brightly painted as the front door. The man was already hurrying off ahead, through a door painted the colour of cherries.

After a short pause, they scurried after him. On the other side of the cherry door, they found themselves in a kitchen, a sweet, plummy smell filling the air. The man was standing on a stool, leaning over an enormous vat of bubbling red liquid.

'JAM!' he shouted. 'If you're wondering. It's jam!'

He dunked the wooden spoon in and carried on stirring, his beard safely wrapped around his neck.

Ember wondered how many times he'd accidentally dipped his beard into his jam before learning to tuck it away like that.

'Sorry to bother you when you're making jam,' said Ember, as politely as she could, 'but we're looking for a—'

'MAP!' shouted the man. 'I knew someone would come one day; I had hoped it would be a devilishly charming fellow. Not to worry, though.'

Hans stepped forward, hands on hips. 'Excuse me. I think I am more than devilishly charming.'

The man looked down and shrugged but there was a smile tugging at one corner of his mouth. 'I'd say you're less charming and more . . . HANDsome!'

The man erupted into laughter so loud, Ember jumped. Hans burst into fits of giggles, and soon the pair were doubled over with bouts of laughter. *His jokes are about as good as Hans*', thought Ember.

The man stopped laughing as suddenly as he had begun and returned to his pot.

'So, can we have it?' said Falcon.

The man ignored him, kept stirring, and then sighed. Finally, he switched off the stove and wiped his hands on his trousers.

'You know,' he said, looking at Falcon. 'It's rude not to ask someone their name when they invite you into their home.' He straightened up and unwrapped his long beard from his neck.

'I am Oaken Swallowson, pleased to meet you.'

Ember introduced herself and her friends and tried not to look as impatient as she felt.

'Right-O,' said Oaken. 'Follow me.'

He led them back through to the hallway and up the staircase, each step creaking as they went. On the wall, photo frames were hung at wonky angles, faces staring out from black and white pictures.

Ember took a closer look at one, a faded photo in a bright purple frame. A younger Oaken, with a beard that only reached his collarbone, was standing with a pair of binoculars and a walking cane, as though he was heading off on an adventure.

'Those were the good old days,' Oaken said wistfully.

He was smiling brightly in all the other photographs, though the people around him were barely smiling at all. Instead, they seemed surprised by the camera, as though Oaken had met them on his travels and immediately ambushed them for a photograph.

They reached the top of the stairs, and the many rooms Ember had been expecting turned out instead to be one large attic, with walls that bent to one side like the roof on the outside had done.

'Mr Swallowson,' said Falcon. 'How did you get the Ever Map in the first place?'

'Please, Oaken is fine.' Oaken strolled over to the other side of the attic, and knelt down next to a trunk. 'Come, come, sit, sit, sit,' he said, gesturing.

They did, and Oaken pulled the trunk towards him. 'How did I get the map, you ask? Well, maybe you've heard of a relative of mine. I daresay you have, given that you share a name,' he said to Hans.

'You're—'

'Correct,' said Oaken, as he clicked the locks on the

204

trunk open and lifted the lid. 'Hans Christof Sanderson was my great-great-grandfather. My mother used to love reading me and my sister his stories before bed, although my father hated them. Eventually, he forbade her from telling them at all, but the secrecy just added to the mystery for me. So, I decided to run away and travel to Mount Ever myself. I must have been no more than eleven years old.'

Oaken lowered his voice as he continued, telling his story as though it were a tale to share around a campfire.

'There were gates and fences and signs surrounding the mountain, warning walkers of dangerous rocks, animals, and deadly sinkholes. Of course, I didn't believe any of *that*. Those are only there to stop anyone from getting too nosy, that's all. Have you heard of the S.E.C.R.E.T. society?'

'Yes,' said Ember.

'The fences were their work, trying to keep the mountains safe, and quite right of them, too. Of course, I climbed Mount Ever anyway.'

He leaned forward and looked directly at Hans.

'You, my handsome friend, are made from mountain

magic, are you not?' he asked.

Hans nodded. 'I'm from Mount Never,' he said.

Oaken sniffed and offered a sad smile. 'That must be quite a lonely life, no? I doubt there are many clock hands like you hopping around?'

For once, Hans didn't say a word. He simply looked down at his hands. *Poor Hans*, thought Ember.

'Sadly, I've never been to Mount Never,' continued Oaken. 'Though I *have* started writing to a new friend who lives there.'

For a moment, Ember thought about asking who. Maybe Flint had been delivering the letters between them. The way villages seemed to be connecting now was incredible, and the prospect of a relationship with this fascinating, invention-filled city, was exciting. But Oaken was already continuing his story, so she put the thought aside for now.

'I found this map, hidden on Mount Ever,' he explained. 'I didn't want to leave it behind. It was reckless, but I wanted some sort of memento from the adventure. I told myself I was keeping it safe, but, really, I couldn't bear to let it go.'

He pulled a tube from the trunk, long and thin like

206

the one Ember's map was kept in. 'If you knew about S.E.C.R.E.T.,' said Falcon, 'why didn't you join them?'

Oaken let out a short laugh. 'I don't think I'd be welcome there, now would I?'

Ember, Hans and Falcon all looked back at him blankly.

'Oh come on, put the two and the two together and make four!' he said. 'You know who Hans Christof Sanderson was . . .'

'A storyteller,' said Ember, bewildered.

'And how did he discover all the things he wrote stories about, do you think? He explored, discovered new landscapes, wrote it all down. Hans Christof Sanderson was . . .'

'The *founder* of S.E.C.R.E.T.?' guessed Ember, realising the truth all of a sudden.

'Correct. After him, my great-grandfather was a director, then my grandfather . . . he was Eden Swallowson, the infamous director who put Moira in charge of Mount Never. Understandably S.E.C.R.E.T. hasn't wanted much to do with my relatives since then.'

No one said a word.

Eventually, Oaken let out a chortle and broke the

silence. 'Though I do have a lot of Grandpa Eden's old files, which make for some interesting reading!' he said with a mischievous wink. 'Anyway, here you go.'

He pushed the tube towards Ember. Even though this was exactly what she'd wanted, she paused. 'Why are you trusting us with it?' she asked. 'You don't even know us.'

'You're children,' Oaken said, simply, as though that were explanation enough.

'But adults are more—' started Ember.

'Adults are overrated,' said Oaken, waving his hand. 'How many adults have believed in legends before seeing proof? Only a handful, if that. But children believe a legend because they *know* it's true. They know, deep down, that some things in this world can't be explained away by science or grown-up talk.'

He paused and looked at Ember. 'How many times have you heard a grown-up say, "I saw a flash of light from the corner in my eye, and maybe, just maybe, it's something magical. Something beyond what we already understand"?'

He waited, but no one responded.

'Never,' he said. 'Grown-ups want to find a logical explanation for anything.'

'But why does that mean you trust us with the map?' asked Ember, confused.

'Because as children, you have infinite potential. You can choose what you want to be, how you want to act, what is real, true, and right. Adults are already too far gone to change. It's the *children* who will make the difference in this world, not the old farts.'

At the word *fart*, Hans broke into a fit of laughter, and Ember grinned. She took the Ever Map from Oaken, and her whole body seemed to relax, relief sweeping over her like a wave. They had it!

Oaken sat upright and shrieked. 'MY JAM!' he shouted. 'If I don't get it into the fridge right away it will spoil!' He leapt to his feet and hurried towards the stairs. 'Come down when you're ready.'

Once he had gone, Ember rolled out the Ever Map alongside the three they had brought with them. They were each remarkably similar in their shapes and layout, but the tiny illustrations covering each mountain were different. Rather than the dirt path that had climbed Mount Never, Ever seemed to be home to a path of tiny, patterned rugs, each one making up a new piece of the path. The clouds representing Never's thick, marshmallow fog had been replaced with wispy plumes of smoke, dotted with tiny flowers suggesting it might be a scented mist, or maybe incense. The building teetering on the peak of the mountain was much more elaborate, with arched windows and a mosaic pattern on its walls.

Mount Sometimes and When were different, too. Sometimes had a brick path with high walls and stained-glass windows, while everything on When seemed metallic, golds and silvers lining the route to a gilded building.

Ember leaned back as she tried to take it all in.

She couldn't believe it. They had done it. Now, they only had to take these four maps back to S.E.C.R.E.T., and they could find the Lost Desert of Time.

'How do they work?' asked Falcon, peering at the maps. 'Now that they're all together, aren't they supposed to show where the desert is?'

'I'm not sure,' Ember said. Slowly, she turned them over, and the corner of two maps brushed together. As they touched, a golden glow spread from where they made contact, then disappeared as they broke apart.

She and Falcon looked at each other, eyes wide. Carefully, Ember pulled the compass device from the Never Map, so the inky illustration disappeared from the back. Then, she put all of the maps face-down and started to lay them together, guided by the golden glow when the edges joined. Finally, with the Never Map at the top, Sometimes below, Ever and When either side, an image appeared across the backs of all four maps.

The legends were true.

A golden shape cut across the space, lines criss-crossing and tangling together. It didn't look like a route though, more like spider webs layered on top of one another.

'I don't know how to read it,' Ember said, frowning as she studied the new lines.

'That's OK,' said Hans. 'They'll be able to figure it out at S.E.C.R.E.T.!'

With a loud whoop, he leapt into the air above them. 'We did it!' he yelled, sailing over to the window. He threw his hands on to the glass and shouted through the pane. 'Hey everybody, we're going to find the Lost Desert!'

Ember giggled and got to her feet, joining him at the window. It was beginning to seem possible that they really *could* find the Lost Desert – and then maybe even turn back time and stop the Thread-Cutter before they ever cut a single thread.

'I still can't believe we've actually done it!' she said. She scooped Hans up into a hug and he laughed happily. 'Anise won't have to destroy all the memories. Once we take the maps back to S.E.C.R.E.T., they will help us fix everything. Right, Falcon?'

But Falcon didn't respond.

Ember turned. 'Falcon?'

The room was empty.

Suddenly, a door slammed downstairs.

Ember let out a cry and turned back to the window. There, beneath them, was Falcon, holding four thin tubes and sprinting down the road ahead. He looked back, just long enough to lock eyes with Ember, who stood paralysed with shock, staring out of the window like a statue.

Then, he turned down an alleyway, and was gone.

16

Ember turned back to the room, confirming her worst fears.

All four maps had gone. Only her backpack remained.

'What's going on?' said Hans. 'Where's Falcon going?'

'He's . . . he's taken the maps.' Ember said it calmly, even though inside she felt sick with dread. 'We have to go. Now.'

Ember grabbed her bag and sprinted down the stairs, Hans following her as fast as he could.

'Oaken, thank you for everything, we're leaving now!' she shouted, hurrying through the hallway.

'OK,' he called from the kitchen. 'Tell Ms Daylands I'll have the file she wants next week!'

Ember stopped in her tracks. She looked at Hans.

'What?' she said, as Oaken walked through to them.

'She reached out to our mayor weeks ago,' he said. 'Said your town has been having difficulty living without the cards and asked if any of us could help you adjust. As soon as I heard, I got in touch and told her who I was, and that I had all these old files about the Fate Mountains, and that maybe I could help and . . .' He trailed off, confused at the expression on Ember's face. 'Ms Daylands was ever so interested in anything about the Threads of Fate, how they could have been manipulated, what power they had . . .'

It felt as though Ember's blood had turned to ice.

Ms Daylands not wanting to do anything hasty to stop the Thread-Cutter . . . Falcon taking the maps . . . Her interest in the threads . . .

Had *Ms Daylands* been cutting threads? Was Falcon somehow helping her? None of it made sense.

Jasper's words flashed in her mind. *Can you really trust your own judgement? Didn't Moira lure you up the mountain?*

Without another word, she pulled Hans into her arms and bolted out the door.

The city seemed to be alive around them. Hans clung to her shoulder as she ran through the narrow streets, forcing her way past people, scanning for a boy clutching an armful of maps. Falcon could have gone anywhere—

No. He would surely be heading for the city gates. Ember ran towards them.

How could she have been so stupid? The secrecy about his name and his village . . . she knew there had been something off about him, and yet she'd trusted him anyway.

Ember and Hans reached the city gates. But as she stood, staring out into the fields that surrounded them, over the homes of the exiled people whose lives had already been destroyed so many times, Ember couldn't see a trace of Falcon.

Nothing.

He had gone.

With all four maps.

But why?

Ember battled with a terrible, awful thought growing in her head. She pushed it aside, wishing it would disappear.

'Ember,' Hans whispered, and she looked down at him in her jacket, knowing he was going to say her horrible thought out loud. 'Is . . . Falcon the Thread-Cutter?'

Ember couldn't speak. Falcon *couldn't* be the Thread-Cutter. They had laughed together, spent time together. He couldn't have done something so awful. Could he?

'Or do you think . . . Ms Daylands . . . she wanted to know about the threads. Did *she* have something to do with this?' asked Hans, still whispering.

Ember didn't know what to say.

She clung to Hans a little tighter.

She had led Falcon to the maps. Whatever Falcon did now, it would be Ember's fault.

*

Ember and Hans sat with their backs to the city walls.

Ember was consumed with guilt. She had desperately convinced Jasper not to wipe everyone's memories, sure that she'd be able to fix it all.

But she had made things worse. Again.

Choosing to take down Moira had felt like a victory at the time, but ever since, all she seemed to be doing was cleaning up the messes that so-called victory had created. Apart from saving Juniper, it was as though nothing good had come from it at all.

And now, she was stuck.

'What do we do?' she whispered.

Hans reached over and put his hand on her knee. 'I don't know.'

'Should we tell S.E.C.R.E.T.? They might be able to track him somehow . . .'

'There's less than two hours before we were supposed to return with the maps,' Hans whispered. 'If we go back *without* them, S.E.C.R.E.T. might speed up their plan to wipe everyone's memories.'

That was true. Even more worryingly, Ember didn't know what Falcon was planning. He had all four maps now; as soon as he figured out how to read the golden map, he could get to the desert and start manipulating time before Ember and Hans had even made it back to S.E.C.R.E.T.

'We aren't giving up,' said Ember defiantly. 'We have to go after Falcon.'

'But how can we find him?' Hans asked. 'If he's gone to the desert, we can't follow him without the maps.'

Hans was right. They had no hope of following him there without the maps.

Unless . . .

'The book,' she said. 'We can read what it says about the desert.'

Hans quickly pulled it out of the bag. Ember flicked it open to the page about the desert. She began to read, as fast as she possibly could without tripping over the words.

Long, long ago, Time was nothing but a grain of sand.

She travelled across the world, cruising its empty plains and deep oceans. Time longed for meaning. She wished she could learn and grow.

Then, one day, Time came across a river.

The river was so bright and clear and blue that

Time saw her reflection in the water. The river saw how happy this made her, and so the river gave Time her reflection.

Now, there were two grains of sand.

Time and her new friend were happy, and the river was pleased. So, the river continued to produce more and more grains of sand, until, eventually, the river dried up. Where it had flowed was now a desert so vast, it seemed to never end.

Time realised that with so many grains of sand, she could do anything. She could turn the planet, she could make the moon come at night, and the sun come during the day. By counting the grains of sand, she could measure how long had passed between the two.

And so, Time grew from a single grain of sand to become the most powerful force in the world.

Seconds grew into minutes, which grew into hours, days, weeks, months, and years.

Soon, Time was busy, and so the Fate Mountains rose to help her. They created people and watched over them, while Time kept the world ticking.

But as the humans filled themselves with knowledge, they began to explore. Time knew that people craved power and control, for it was the way the mountains had made them. She knew that before she had ticked many more tocks, someone would try to control her.

So Time hid her desert. She pulled every grain of sand below the surface and hid her powers at the centre of it all.

Her location would remain a mystery for ever, safe from the prying eyes of people everywhere.

It is said only Fate knows her location, as Fate knows all things.

Hans was listening intently.

'It doesn't tell us how to get there,' Ember said, and sighed.

Hans sank back and sat on his hands. 'But the explorers who *made* the maps must have found the desert once. Surely we can too?'

'Maybe there's someone we can ask,' Ember said, her mind ticking. She read the last line of the story again. '*Fate knows all things.* Perhaps that means the Fate Mountains. But we can't ask the mountains.'

She paused for a second, thinking about the stories and all the connections between them. They were web-like, each one crossing the next . . .

'The spiders!' she shouted. 'They must know all about Fate; they make the *Threads* of Fate!'

'YES!' yelled Hans, whooping and cheering in the air. 'Let's go!'

Ember bundled the book back into the bag and the pair of them began running back the way they had come.

Who knew where Falcon was by now? Would he make it to the desert before they even made it back to Mount Never? It was a long journey back, but it was the only choice they had. *Maybe May will know a faster route*, thought Ember hopefully.

After re-crossing the field to the tunnel entrance, they got their tickets checked, and jumped into a mine cart, holding on tight as it rattled through the tunnel.

All the excitement Ember had felt earlier in their journey was gone. It seemed so silly now that she had been excited at all.

Silly to have trusted Falcon, and silly to have ever thought her plan would be better than S.E.C.R.E.T.'s. She had made so many mistakes.

And if she didn't catch Falcon before he made it to the desert, the whole world might have to pay for them.

221

'Ember? Hans?' May said, as they climbed through the trapdoor to the Emocean. 'Back already! Where's Falcon?'

'So he didn't come through here?' asked Ember.

'No, why would he?'

Ember and Hans exchanged a glance. That must mean the desert was another way. 'He stole the maps. All of them.'

May's face dropped. 'No!' she said.

'We thought he was our friend,' said Hans.

May smiled kindly. 'I'm sorry, Hans. Sometimes, people aren't who they seem to be.'

'We think we have a plan,' said Ember. 'We might be able to get to the Desert of Time first, even without the maps. But we need to get to Everspring, *fast*.'

May looked at them both carefully, and then crouched down. 'You really think you can find the desert and stop Falcon?'

Hans leapt forwards. 'Absolutely, Miss May,' he said. 'We will do everything we can. Even though we sort of messed up already and kind of didn't do the job we said we would do and—'

'Is there a faster way to get back to Everspring than the way we came?' interrupted Ember.

May shook her head. 'I'm sorry, you came through the fastest route.'

'Isn't there a secret super speedy tunnel that can take us anywhere?' asked Hans. 'Like a wormhole? Or a special coral that zaps us wherever we need to go?'

'Sorry,' said May. 'Although that would be rather convenient, wouldn't it?'

She frowned, and Ember recognised her own thinking expression in May's face.

'Are you double-sure?' asked Hans hopefully.

'I'm sure there's no faster route . . .' said May slowly. 'But maybe we can speed up the route we *do* have. We're inventors, aren't we?' she asked. 'Maybe together, we can speed up the tunnel's mechanisms.'

Ember's heart quickened. Working with May to improve a S.E.C.R.E.T. invention? 'That would be great!'

'We'd better get started then,' said May. She rushed to the other side of the glass igloo and, from behind the armchair, pulled out a large briefcase. 'Trusty toolbox,' she said.

Ember reached into her own bag and pulled out her own, thrilled to have a similar kit.

'Here's what I don't understand,' said May as they made their way towards the walkway. 'Why would Falcon want to go to the Desert of Time alone?'

'Because he's the Thread-Cutter,' said Ember bitterly, but even as she said it, she realised it didn't make sense. Why would the Thread-Cutter want to go to the Desert? There were no Threads of Fate there . . . And if Falcon wasn't the Thread-Cutter, did that leave Ms Daylands as their prime suspect?

May stopped in her tracks for a moment. She closed her eyes and brought her hand to her face. 'Oh my goodness,' she said. 'Jasper told me something.'

'What? What is it?' said Ember.

'He did some . . . digging on the three of you, once you'd left, to check that he could trust you. He found that Falcon was . . . well, he was banished from his village when he received his Fate Card.'

Ember sighed and closed her eyes. *Of course.* Falcon didn't have a name or a village *any more.* She remembered the way Falcon had acted around the other people who had been banished, like he didn't want anyone to recognise him.

'That's . . . awful,' said Ember. No wonder he didn't want Anise to wipe the memories. If she had, he would believe he had *chosen* to leave his family and be alone.

'If he wants to turn back time, he might be trying to turn it back all the way to before he even got his Fate Card,' said May. 'But that . . . that could have horrific consequences.'

Ember was torn between sadness for Falcon, and fear at the thought of what turning back so much time might do. She had no idea what age he had received his card. It could have been years ago . . .

'Come on,' said May. 'If we're right, we need to hurry.'

May rushed to the start of the walkway and popped open a panel on the floor.

Inside were the mechanics: the motor, resistor, brake panel – all parts Ember had read about but never seen in this exact set-up and combination.

Ember suddenly felt very out of her depth.

'Do you know how the tunnel transport works?' May asked.

'This one is a conveyor belt, but I don't know about the others,' said Ember.

May smiled mischievously. 'They're *all* conveyor belts. The river water is pulled along on a belt that attracts water, and the baskets are pulled along by a conveyor belt topped with mud Anise created, using a chemical reaction,' she explained. 'They all have the same basic mechanisms, it's just the design that is different.'

Ember nodded, amazed. Mixing engineering with science sounded fantastic, and she was desperate to ask more about the chemical reactions, but they didn't have time.

'So, this is the control panel for the walkway?' asked Ember.

'Yes, but there isn't a control that speeds things up,' said May. 'There's a resistor which keeps it at the same speed.'

They studied it in silence. Then, 'What about removing the resistor?' Ember suggested hesitantly.

'Good idea!' said May. 'Although removing it might make it too dangerous to ride. But how about . . .'

May reached in with a screwdriver and twisted a bolt on the resistor.

'Let's see if turning the resistor down slightly works.' She pushed the panel closed, and together the three of them gingerly stepped on to the walkway.

Suddenly, it jerked to life. Ember grabbed hold of Hans and crouched down, gripping the handrail tightly as the walkway gathered speed. May did the same, grabbing the rail on the other side.

Wind began to whip past them, and Ember felt her face distort with the force. She looked over to May, whose lips and cheeks were flapping at the sides. If they weren't in such a panic, it would have been funny.

Ember clung to the handrail as the walkway whizzed them through the ocean, past all the fish and the flashes of colourful animals.

Despite its incredible speed, the walkway still didn't feel fast enough.

Every second that passed was a second Falcon might be getting closer to the desert.

Soon, the walkway slowed down and ahead, the steps up to the Tremoring Tropics awaited. But as it came to a halt, Ember couldn't help worrying . . . was it soon enough?

17

'Come on!' said Hans, as they ran up the steps to the Tremoring Tropics. 'Let's go talk to the spiders!'

As he jumped up the last step, Ember turned back to May, who was still standing at the end of the walkway.

'You're not coming?' asked Ember. She had felt a little more confident having May with them.

'No, I need to warn Jasper,' she said quietly. 'If Falcon is planning what we think he is, then Anise needs to get to Cloud Memory as soon as possible.'

Ember swallowed, imagining Anise and Jasper's disappointment in her. But there was no time for regrets, not yet anyway.

'Ember,' May said, very seriously. 'I truly hope you stop Falcon and save the Thread-Cutter's victims *before* Anise wipes the memories. You *can* do this. Remember, you can change all the transports through the tunnels as we did now. The next tunnel might appear to be a log boat, but the water runs on a track like my walkway.'

'OK,' Ember said, though she didn't feel it.

They said goodbye and Ember turned, once again avoiding the jaws of the hungry-looking plant. With Hans in his usual spot tucked in her jacket, she set off through the rainforest. They skirted the edge of the clearing, where Nimbo was still shouting orders at the mon-keys, although it seemed as though they were all having much more fun now.

Eventually, Ember came to the end of the river, where the log boat waited. Once they had located the hidden panel controlling the water, Ember popped it open just as May had done with the panel by the walkway.

Carefully, she twisted the resistor, not too far, and bit her lip. Hopefully, she had done it right.

Next to the panel, partly hidden by vines over the forest floor, was their ticket checker. Hans and Ember slipped the tickets inside, waited for them to be returned, and then boarded the log boat.

Immediately the water surged forwards, waves splashing up around them, and Ember clutched Hans closer.

'AaahhAAAhhhAHAHHHH!' shouted Hans as the log sped up, bumping along the sides of the riverbank.

'Hold on!' shouted Ember.

The speed they hurtled forwards at seemed out of control. They were flying up into the air, then smashing down on to the water again, zipping along the channel out of the rainforest and into the fields, along the hills, all at incredible speed.

Ember's stomach rattled as the water sloshed around them; every time they turned or dipped down, the water would splash up and cover them in an almighty wave until they were soaked from head to toe, shivering in the cold.

It will be over soon. It will be over soon! Ember thought, trying to keep calm as the log rocketed along the track.

And then, with one last plummet down into the darkness underground, the log slowed down, and finally, they were back in Everspring.

Ember leapt from the log with Hans in her arms.

'Eurgh!' said Hans, as he wiped himself down. 'Didn't expect that!'

'At least you can get dry quickly,' said Ember, her

teeth chattering. It was *freezing!* And there was nothing she could do about her drenched clothes. 'Never mind, come on.'

They sprinted through the forest. Ember noticed the sun had begun to sink over the tops of the trees. Mount Never was up ahead. Then they could ask the spiders and—

'Ember?!'

A voice broke through the air.

Hans stopped a few steps ahead of her, and Ember crashed into him.

'JUNIPER!' Hans shouted, bouncing up to hug Ember's sister.

Juniper did *not* look happy. She stood, arms folded, frowning at them. 'Where have you been? Everyone's been asking me, and Ms Daylands has been flying off the handle—'

'What has she said?' Ember said, gripping both of Juniper's shoulders. 'Ms Daylands. What did she say?'

'Only that you're in trouble, and she's worried about you . . .'

'Did she say anything about someone called Oaken? Is Falcon here?' Ember couldn't stop the questions tumbling out.

Juniper shook her head. 'No and no. Why don't you come and talk to Ms Daylands?'

'Ms Daylands is still in Everspring?' Ember frowned. Ms Daylands had told her yesterday that she would be going away.

Juniper nodded slowly as if Ember had hit her head or something. 'Of course she is. Like I said, she's worried about you.'

Ember didn't know what to think. Ms Daylands' interest in the Threads of Fate, her connection to Oaken, her secrecy over her whereabouts . . . it was still possible she was the Thread-Cutter.

Ember wished they had more time to find the answers, but right now, they had to focus on stopping Falcon.

'Look,' started Ember. 'We think Falcon is doing something terrible, and we have to stop him. I'm worried Ms Daylands might be doing terrible things as well, but I don't know for sure. We don't have time to explain anything else. Sorry, Juniper.'

She turned away from her sister and grabbed Hans' hand.

'Maybe I can help!' said Juniper, following behind.

'Wait here and I'll tell you everything later.' *If I still remember it all*, thought Ember.

'NO!' shouted Juniper. 'No I won't wait here!'

Ember turned, shocked by Juniper's outburst.

Her sister, red in the face, was glaring back at her. 'Do you have any idea how unfair this is?' Juniper shouted. 'Ever since you destroyed Moira's machine and the cards to save my life, I've been shut out by everyone – I don't need it from my own sister! Do you know how awful it is to hear everyone say how much they hate their new life, all because I got saved? I'm grateful for what you did, but what's the point of it if even *you* don't want to spend any time with me!'

Ember looked at her sister, taken aback. 'I was just trying to protect—'

'You didn't even want me to come into the mountain yesterday, but *I* was the one who stopped Lacey from webbing us up!' she cried.

'I'm sorry, I—'

'Maybe start thinking about how I might be able to *help*, rather than leaving me out of things.'

Ember looked at Hans. Hans stared back, tiny eyebrows raised expectantly.

She turned back to her sister. It was true; everyone had been keeping Juniper at arm's length since she had escaped death. Ember had been one of the worst culprits, acting like Juniper still might die at any moment.

That wasn't fair – not any fairer than everyone treating *her* as if the struggles after the Fate Cards were her fault.

She sighed. 'Fine, come on. We're going to see the spiders. We'll explain on the way.'

With an excited squeal, Juniper's anger disappeared. As they hurried along, Hans explained everything that had happened so far.

*

When they reached the centre of the mountain, Ember realised that things were different inside the spiders' domain. The last time there had been no threads moving around, but now they were everywhere, bouncing along the floor. The spiders were scurrying around in a sea of threads.

'What's going on?' asked Hans.

'Lacey!' called Juniper, running forward into the throng.

Ember and Hans hurried after her.

'You three again,' said Lacey, although with a hint of affection. 'You've caught us at a busy moment. These Threads of Fate are alive and ready to be sent out into the mountain's realms. It's a bit hectic in here.'

She paused, shook free a tiny blue thread that had wrapped itself around her front right leg, and looked at Ember.

'Did you find anything on the mountain?' she asked.

Ember nodded. 'Threads are being cut,' she whispered. Lacey gasped, but Ember continued. 'We're trying to stop the person who's doing it. But first we need to find the Lost Desert of Time. Do you know anything about it?'

Suddenly, the whole mountain went quiet.

Every single spider stopped spinning their threads, speaking, or scuttling, and every pair of eyes was on Ember.

'You told me you were good people,' Lacey growled.

'We are,' Ember said, confused. 'Why do you think we aren't?'

Lacey stepped forward, past Juniper. 'Because anyone who wants to find the Lost Desert is only after one thing: to control time.'

'No, we—'

'And we are sworn protectors of both the mountains and the desert,' said Lacey, advancing on Ember. Ember didn't feel as though they were around friends any more. It was very quiet, tense, and the sight of a cocoon of web in the corner of her eye made her shudder.

Lacey edged forward threateningly. 'I should have dealt with you last time you came here. Now threads are being cut . . .'

The spider took another step forward, and then raised her two front legs.

'I know, and we're . . . We're trying . . .' said Ember, struggling to find the right words as Lacey stepped closer and closer, an awful look on her face.

'Lacey, wait,' said Juniper, calmly placing her hand on Lacey's front leg. 'Let me explain.'

Ember watched as one of Lacey's eyes rested on Juniper, before her legs went down. 'Quickly,' she said.

The rest of the spiders seemed to take that as a signal to hurry up and get back to work, and so the mountain began to hum again with noise.

'A boy called Falcon has all four of the Fate Mountain maps,' said Juniper, retelling the story Hans had just told her. 'We don't know exactly what he is going to do, but we think he wants to turn back time . . . dangerously far into the past,' she said, and then looked at Ember to check she was recounting it correctly.

Lacey turned. 'I told you,' she said to Ember. 'If you hadn't killed Moira, then we wouldn't be in this mess in the first place.'

She was right.

'I . . .' But Ember didn't know what to say.

'But we're trying to help,' said Hans cheerily. 'We're helpers!'

Lacey let out a deep breath, her whole body rising and falling above her legs. 'Fine,' she said. 'But hear me, Ember Shadows. If you do something that puts us in danger, I will come for you and your silly little clock hand. There's nothing more important to me than keeping this mountain safe.'

Ember met the spider's eyes bravely. 'That's important to me, too. I promise.'

The spider considered her for a moment, and gave a slow nod.

'Then come with me,' said Lacey. 'There's an entrance to the Desert of Time here.'

'There is?' asked Ember, hardly daring to believe her luck. Hans did a somersault.

'Of course,' said Lacey. 'The mountains have been linked to the desert since the beginning of time. There's an entrance deep inside each of the Fate Mountains.'

She turned and walked into the sea of spiders, followed by Ember, Juniper and Hans, and the crowd parted for them.

As they walked further into the mountain, Ember desperately fought the guilt in her chest. Ember hadn't lied to Lacey; but she hadn't told the whole truth either. Lacey didn't know that Ember herself wanted to turn back time to save the Thread-Cutter's victims. It might not be as dangerous as what they believed Falcon had planned, but Ember did still hope to control time.

She wanted to be honest but knew that if Lacey found out, she would never show them the desert. So instead, Ember decided to choose her words carefully.

'Will it be easy for Falcon to turn back time?' she asked.

'No,' said Lacey. 'I do not even know how such a thing would be done. But no one knew how to trap fates, until Moira. There is always a way, and someone determined enough will always find it.' They had arrived at the end of the tunnel, and Lacey carefully pulled aside a web to reveal a hidden door.

'We won't let anything bad happen, I promise,'

Ember said, turning to Juniper and Hans. 'Ready?'

But as they stepped through the door, Ember's chest tightened.

Despite her promise, she had no idea how they were going to stop Falcon.

18

The tunnel was black as a crow's feathers. Ember's Illumitube only gave them a few metres of glowing light, but it was something.

There was no S.E.C.R.E.T. transport to speed them along, no lamps along the walls, and so Ember, Hans and Juniper simply hurried through the dark tunnel, holding on to one another to stay together.

It was unnerving. Ember squeezed Juniper's hand, knowing how much her sister had always hated the darkness.

Slowly, the air in the tunnel changed. It became dusty, warm, and humid. The ground shifted strangely under her feet and Ember realised it was sand beneath her Shh!-Oos.

They must be close.

As they continued, light started to seep in from up ahead and it grew warmer and warmer, until Ember no longer shivered beneath her wet clothes. She nearly went to peel off her jacket, but she always needed somewhere for Hans to stay safe, so kept it on. The faint light grew into a sort of moonlit glow, until, eventually, they began to see shapes ahead.

The tunnel came to an end.

Ahead was a space so large and so vast that Ember couldn't take it all in.

The Lost Desert of Time.

Ember squeezed Hans a little closer. All this time, explorers had thought they needed maps and cryptic clues, when all they truly needed was to speak to the spiders, build a friendship, and earn their trust as Juniper had done. Friendship really did mean everything.

The desert lay ahead of them, stretching out to the horizon in all directions. It seemed never-ending, dunes in the distance as large as mountains, and an impossible night sky hanging above them despite being deep underground. Stars lit the space around them, brightly shining down on the magical landscape that had been hidden for centuries. A group of stars formed a crack-like shape in the sky, and purple and blue light seeped from the crack into the darkness around it.

Immediately where the tunnel ended, something – or someone – had laid out small white lanterns on the ground, tiny flames in each one. The lanterns, Ember realised, were marking the edge of a path. They appeared to lead towards a strange collection of buildings, arranged so that each building was like a point on a star. Even more buildings were scattered in the desert beyond. She couldn't properly see them all, but Ember could make out some of the closest buildings: a lighthouse tower, a circular tent, small huts, and then, in the far distance, a larger white marble building with three domes on its roof. Beyond that was an enormous dune, towering higher than any other around it.

Despite the beauty of the place, the buildings, and the lanterns, there wasn't a single sound.

'Come on,' said Juniper. 'We need to be quick, don't we?'

'But where should we search?' whispered Hans, clearly shocked by the enormity of the desert. 'Falcon could be anywhere.'

'Let's try the closest buildings first,' said Ember.

They set off on the lantern-lined path, the sand

unstable beneath their feet, and quickly came to the first building: the lighthouse tower, made from what looked like rocks. Outside, there was a small signpost, yellow emblazoned with white words.

Lost and Found

'Why would there be a lost and found *here*?' said Ember.

'Let's have a look,' said Hans. 'If we can climb up to the top of the tower, we might be able to see where Falcon is.'

Ember nodded. As she pushed the dark brown door, sand fell between her fingers as though the door – which looked like wood – was made of nothing more than sand.

Hans looked up at her, and she tried to ignore the concerned look on his face. It did feel creepy here, but they couldn't worry about that. They had to find Falcon.

As they entered the tower, Ember realised with a flicker of disappointment that climbing it would be impossible; there were no steps. Instead, the brick walls were lined with shelves, spanning all the way around the circular space, right up to the top. On the shelves were thousands and thousands of hourglasses, each one filled with a different amount of sand. Strangely, in some, the sand had settled in the bottom of the glass; but in others, it was suspended at the top, somehow not filtering down to the bottom. Each had an inscription on it, written on a tiny plaque.

'Four minutes,' Ember read. 'Lost by Ivy Miller, who couldn't work out how it had taken so long to tie her shoes.'

She moved over to another. 'Twelve seconds, found by Elm Spices, who managed to complete her homework ahead of schedule.'

Each one had a different scenario on it – someone who had lost time in their day, or found a few minutes or seconds. 'Ember, look at this one,' said Juniper.

Ember rushed over and read the inscription aloud. 'Eight months. Lost by Falcon Sky, who could have spent the time with his twin sister Peregrine, had he not been banished on the arrival of his Fate Card.'

For a moment, everything seemed to stand still around her as the pieces clicked into place.

No wonder Falcon was trying to control time. Ember knew how awful it was to be apart from Juniper, and he hadn't seen his twin for eight months. Of course he wanted to turn things back to before he received his Fate Card. Ember understood – there were things she wished she could undo too. But not if it meant putting everyone else in danger.

'Come on, we have to get to Falcon before it's too late,' she said.

Stepping outside the Lost and Found, Ember expected to find the desert exactly as it had been on their way in. But as her foot hit the ground, the sand beneath gave way.

She cried out but was already sliding, whooshing down a dune, the sand crashing around her like a wave, pulling her deeper down. Ember scrabbled and scrambled to hold on to something, but there was nothing, just sand between her fingers. She kept falling, Juniper speeding past her, clutching Hans.

Ember reached out, touching his metal fingers, but they were gone again before she could grip them.

And, just as the sand was threatening to rise up to her chin, it suddenly stopped moving.

She pulled herself free and slid the remaining distance to the bottom of the dune, looking around for the others. But they weren't there.

'Hans!' she shouted. Frantically, she began digging. 'Juniper!'

Hans' head popped up a few metres away, followed by Juniper's.

Ember breathed a sigh of relief.

'Eurgh yuck!' Hans said, and spat a mouthful of sand out ahead of him.

But a mouthful of sand was the least of their problems. The stars illuminating the desert were now very far away. They were in a canyon, deep in a pit of sand.

'No!' Ember shouted. 'How are we going to get out of here?'

The canyon seemed to stretch all the way ahead of her and far behind, and the wall was so steep there was no way they would be able to climb it; especially not when the sand kept moving and sliding beneath their feet.

No sooner had the thought crossed her mind, than she heard a rumbling behind her. She looked, barely daring to imagine what was going to happen next.

Flying towards them, gathering momentum with

every second, was a wave of sand, building and building as high as the canyon walls themselves. And it was hurtling straight towards them.

She reached out and grabbed Hans, pulling him close. Juniper's face flashed with fear and she grabbed Ember's other hand as the wave swept them up. Ember squeezed Juniper's hand, desperately trying to keep hold of both her and Hans as the wave carried them forwards. Sand pulled them under, then back to the surface and under again as they hurtled forward, all the way along the canyon.

Suddenly, the wave beneath them surged, pushing higher and higher, until it spat them out, and they landed on the side of the canyon, each of them flat on their backs and staring up at the sky.

Sand stuck to Ember's hair and damp clothes, scratching at her eyes and filling her ears.

She didn't like this desert, not a single bit. Time was *completely* unpredictable.

'That was *horrible*,' said Juniper, shaking herself clean.

Hans agreed and spat out yet another mouthful of sand. 'Do you think Time feels under attack?'

Ember nodded. 'Maybe.'

She looked back to the Lost and Found and saw that, miraculously, the lanterns lining the path had remained perfectly in place. It was as though there had never been a tidal wave of sand at all. And yet the wave had brought them much further into the desert. Ember glanced around, the desert shapes illuminated by the thousands of stars overhead. To their left was the dome-topped building and, further ahead, the path stretched on and on, straight into the enormous sand dune, which Ember could now see had a small door on the side.

Slightly ahead, at a fork in the path, was a signpost: *Stitches of Time*, *Wasted Time Refuge*, *Free Time* and *The Centre for Healing All Wounds*. But none of them seemed like a place Falcon might have gone to turn back time.

'Where *is* he?' muttered Ember, frustrated.

Panic was beginning to rise in her chest. At this rate, they'd never find Falcon, let alone stop him doing something terrible before S.E.C.R.E.T. took all their magical memories.

Ember glanced at the domed building, which was

now closest to them. It was beautiful, a white marble colour with golden spires on each dome. There, at the arched doorway covered with a purple curtain, she spotted movement; a small, sand-coloured something twitched and them seemed to roll back inside the door.

'Come on,' she said, 'I think I saw something.'

Ember began to run down the lantern-lit path towards the building.

'Wait!' shouted Juniper. 'How do you know it's not a trap? That wave nearly suffocated us; this might be even worse!'

Hans looked up at Ember and back to Juniper. 'We . . . we don't *ever* know, Juniper. But we don't have another choice,' he said.

Ember felt a pang of guilt at Juniper's fearful eyes.

Juniper paused for a moment and then nodded, letting Ember take her hand.

'All right then,' Juniper said. 'Let's go.'

19

Ember reached for the velvet curtain.

With a deep breath and a quick smile to comfort Juniper, she pulled it to one side.

A tiny part of Ember had half-expected to find Falcon here.

Instead, they found a room much smaller than the building suggested. Shelves lined all four walls, and there was a counter running in front of the back wall, where a single, flickering candle sat. Once again, there were hourglasses *everywhere*.

Each one had a different amount of sand in there, and each was slightly different in its design. Ember brushed her fingers against the nearest shelf, and sand particles floated off.

It was as though this whole world was made from sand, even though it *looked* as though it were filled with wood, marble, and glass.

But nowhere in the room was there any sign of the

movement she had seen outside.

'Are you *sure* you saw something?' asked Juniper quietly.

Just then, something sprang from behind the counter and leapt on to its surface, before rolling right along from one side to the other.

'Ta-dah!' it shouted, spreading its hands and feet wide, as though it had put on a show. Then it doubled over, holding its clawed right hand to its side, its strange, long face grimacing in pain.

'Howdy there!' it said, wincing. 'I'm Nick.'

Hans didn't seem to notice the animal's discomfort, and began to applaud. Ember stared at the creature, feeling increasingly hopeless. It wasn't Falcon. How were they *ever* going to find him?

But Juniper stepped forwards. 'Are you hurt?' she asked.

'He said his name was *Nick*, not Hurt!' said Hans, confused.

'That's right,' the creature said. 'Nick of Time.'

Nick's entire body was made from small, tough scales, like armour. His face was narrowed into a snout at the end and, as Ember watched, an incredibly long tongue stretched out, smacked an hourglass on the shelf, spun it round, and then whipped back into its mouth. Ember had just opened her mouth to ask Nick if he seen a young boy anywhere, when Juniper spoke.

'You're a pangolin, aren't you?' asked Juniper. Ember closed her mouth again . . . if anyone could get an animal to help them, it was Juniper.

Her sister continued. 'Pangolins are fabulous creatures, you're nocturnal, and you're able to close up your ears to keep out ants and—'

'And sand!' said Nick. 'You're right. I'm probably the most impressive creature in the whole entire world. Especially since I'm not any old pangolin. I'm a Time Pangolin.'

As he spoke, the scales at the tip of Nick's tail began to ripple, sending a wave all the way through them, over his back and up to his head. As each scale moved, some turned darker, until a shape appeared on his back. Ember blinked. It was a clock – each number was within a single scale of Nick's armoured body in a circle formation, while the thin hands of the clock stretched across a few scales, ticking in time as the seconds passed.

'This is the time, right now, in the farthest depths of the Emocean,' he said proudly. 'Where are you from?'

'Everspring!' shouted Hans, clapping his hands together in excitement.

Nick rippled his scales again and the clock changed to show a new time. 'Ta-dah!'

'Amazing!' said Juniper. 'But how did you get *this* stuck in your side?' Juniper pointed to a small metal thorn sticking out from between his scales.

'I don't know,' he said, sighing, and his scales rippled back to their original sandy colour. 'I'm supposed to be tough but . . .' He trailed off.

Ember opened her mouth to jump in. It wasn't that she didn't care about the poor pangolin, but they had *world-saving* matters to attend to.

But Juniper smiled warmly, shot Ember a glare as

though she knew what she was thinking, and said, 'Don't worry, I'll have it out in a moment.'

Nick's long face lit up and he sat down on the surface of the counter, letting Juniper get to work. Hans jumped up to sit next to him, but as soon as his feet touched the countertop, he slipped right through the sand structure and landed on the ground.

'Can I interest you in a loan?' said Nick, as Juniper looked at the wound. 'I'd be more than happy to offer you a good deal if you want to borrow time. Or maybe you'd like to spend some? How would you like to invest your time today?'

Nick waved his hand at the shelves behind him filled with hourglasses.

'We actually need to find someone,' said Ember quickly, sensing her chance. 'Have you seen a boy running through here?'

'Oh, you mean the one with the four funny tubes?' said Nick. 'He came barging in here, asking me to give him eight months back! Can you imagine?' Nick shook his head. 'Well, I told him, sorry, sir, the only time we can offer here is short-term loans. No more than five minutes I'm afraid.'

'Where did he go?' Ember asked.

Juniper made a sudden movement and yanked the thorn from Nick's side.

'YOUCH!' shouted Nick, hopping to his feet. He looked down at his side, and then back at Juniper with a smile. 'Thank you very much, young lady. Much better! Who are you all anyway?'

Ember chewed her lip impatiently as Juniper made the introductions. As soon as she could, she interrupted.

'The boy – where did he go?' Ember said.

'Not sure. He left, that's all I know. Anyway, I'm offering you the deal of a lifetime here! Invest time wisely and you could reap the benefits. You could borrow, spend, save, whatever you like!' said Nick, clearly giving his best sales presentation.

'OOOH,' said Hans. 'We are trying to *save* time, but not really in the same way . . .'

Juniper stepped towards Nick and smiled kindly. Ember couldn't understand how she managed to remain patient, when her own mind was racing. They needed to chase after Falcon!

'Mr Nick,' said Juniper. 'We do like all of your kind offers, but we have to find that boy.'

Nick tilted his head to the side, his skin rippling with each tile as he did. 'Why?'

'He wants to find out how to *control* time. Maybe even turn it back, way more than five minutes,' said Ember urgently.

'Why didn't you say so?!' shouted Nick, springing to his feet. 'If he controls time . . . well, I'm meant to look after time and . . .'

'Then maybe you can show us where he went?' prompted Juniper.

Nick nodded furiously. 'He was running all over the place. But if he wants to control time, he'll have to go to the large dune; you'll have seen it already. It's the centre of the desert, the place where time ticks.'

'Oh, but if he's already figured out that's where he has to go, we'll never have enough time to catch h—' Ember stopped, her own words giving her the answer. 'Nick, can you give us more time?'

'Isn't that what I've been saying? Only a loan, though. You'll have to give it back,' he said.

'How does it work?' asked Ember.

'Simple. Think of an ordinary person, out there in the world, living their usual day; they move through time quite evenly. Well, we can stop time for them, and squeeze in some extra minutes just for you, between one of their minutes and the next. We do it by using one of these hourglasses.'

Nick stuck his tongue out, pointing at one on the shelf, before sucking it back in. 'But we only do *short*-term loans. Anything longer than five minutes could have disastrous consequences.'

'How do I give the time back to you?' Ember said, confused by the strange exchange.

'Don't worry, I'll take it back from you later. For example, a little task that should take you a minute or two – well, you might look up and find it took ten.' He flicked his tongue out and retrieved an hourglass from the shelf. 'Now, how long do you want?' he asked.

Ember looked at Hans. 'A few minutes should be enough, shouldn't it?' Hans suggested. 'How long ago was Falcon here?'

Nick held up his small hand. 'Three minutes and thirty-five seconds ago. My own little titbit of advice would be take all five,' he said. His scales shifted, and a stopwatch appeared on his back, a single hand counting down. 'If you take five minutes, the world will stop and you might be able to catch up and get there *before* him.'

Ember nodded her agreement and Nick put a hand on the bottom of the hourglass. Sand appeared in the lower section. He passed it to Ember, and then did the same for a second hourglass. He gave that one to Juniper.

'Now, this is important,' he said. 'You have to be touching me *and* the hourglass.'

'Why?' asked Hans, curious.

With a puzzled look, Nick stuck his tongue out and slapped it against Hans.

'Hey!' giggled Hans. 'That tickles!'

'Just as I thought,' said Nick. 'Are you from a magical landscape?'

Hans nodded.

'Like me,' said Nick, happily. 'Time doesn't affect us like it does them. It doesn't have the same control over us. That's why you don't need an hourglass.'

Ember, Juniper and Hans all stared back at him blankly.

He sighed and rolled his tiny eyes. 'The hourglass stops time so it can squeeze in the extra minutes. It doesn't keep you humans from stopping *with* it. But if you're touching me, or Hans, you're safe. You'll be *outside* of time.'

It made a sort of sense. There wasn't a single magical creature or landscape Ember had seen that obeyed the rules of time like people did.

Nick jumped up into Juniper's arms, and Hans did the same with Ember.

'It's set for five minutes. When you're ready, turn it to start. When the hourglass dissolves, you're back in normal time,' said Nick. 'And Juniper, *don't* let go of me. Ember, don't let go of Hans.'

Ember took a deep breath. 'Ready,' she said, 'three . . . two . . . one . . . turn.'

20

'Did it work?' asked Hans.

Ember's hourglass was certainly running, sand pouring from the top chamber into the bottom, and Juniper's was doing the same.

'Of course it did!' shouted Nick. 'Now let's get going!'

It was a strange sort of feeling, Ember thought, being free to move outside of the passage of time. She caught sight of the candle on the counter. It had paused mid-flicker; the flame had frozen, wax stopped mid-drip down the side.

She turned back to see Juniper and Nick waiting at the door, the stopwatch on his back ticking down. 'Four minutes and thirty-five seconds left,' Nick urged. 'Hurry, hurry, hurry!'

Holding on tight to Hans, Ember raced out to the pathway. The dune was far on their right-hand side.

'Juniper, would you sit on the ground for me?'

asked Nick. Juniper gave Ember a puzzled look, but agreed. Nick reached down, waved his nails in front of his face for a moment, and then stuck one arm in the ground.

'What are you do—' began Ember. But she never had time to finish. Because as Nick's nails dug into the sand below, the floor gave way as it had done outside the Lost and Found. This time, it seemed to be at Nick's command. That was little comfort as they fell with the wave of sand, rushing downwards into a canyon.

'AHHHH!' Hans yelled, and the sand dragged them down.

Ember gripped hold of Hans and her hourglass as though her life depended on it. From the corner of Ember's eye, she saw Juniper clinging on to Nick, while screaming at the top of her voice.

The wave continued to push them forward until it jerked them to the right. Nick was controlling the sand, using the desert to help them get them there faster.

'Hold on to your hourglasses!' shouted Nick over Juniper's screams.

The sand swelled beneath them, and Ember could see above ground again. They were getting closer and closer to the giant sand dune with the small door in its front. She clenched her eyes closed as the sand threw them forward on to the ground.

With a thump, they landed in front of the door and Ember jolted upright as quickly as she could, checking she still had hold of Hans and her hourglass, and that Juniper had Nick.

'How long left, Nick?' she asked, tucking Hans into her jacket where he could still touch her arm.

'Two minutes, thirty-seven seconds,' he said.

'Did we go past Falcon?' she asked. 'Did anyone see him?'

Juniper and Hans both shook their heads. 'He could have gone a different way,' said Nick. 'But if he's trying to control time, *this* is where he'll have to come, eventually.'

Ember looked at the door ahead. It was curved at the top, a deep mahogany brown, and had black rounded pieces of iron dotted down the front. She stepped forward and then paused, looking back at Juniper and Hans.

It was Ember's fault they were in this mess, but they were *all* going to have to face what would happen next. She'd learnt a long time ago that most things were harder to do alone. And this, she thought, was bound to be difficult, and probably dangerous.

Ember pushed open the door, feeling more sand beneath her fingers.

A warmth washed over her. The air inside the strange dune was even hotter than outside. She stepped inside with Hans safely tucked in her jacket, feeling the others follow behind her.

Slowly, her eyes adjusted to the new light inside the dune, and she saw . . .

'Careful!' she shouted to Juniper, and just in time.

They were standing right on the edge of a colossal crater. Only a metre or so ahead of them, the ground dropped down into an vast pit below. In the pit stood a giant hourglass, an enormous version of the one Ember held in her hand, but with no lid, and no base. Its glass was planted in the bottom of the pit and it stretched all the way to the roof of the dune. Ember stared up to the middle point of the glass. Incredibly, the sand inside was suspended, not moving at all, each grain glowing like a tiny star.

'Magical, isn't it?' said Nick, his taloned hands

clasped adoringly as he sat in Juniper's arms.

'It's more magical than anything I've ever seen,' said Hans. 'And *I'm* magical!'

Juniper stepped forwards and Ember saw the wonder on her face. Ember smiled, the panic over Falcon subsiding for a moment. She hadn't realised how it would feel to finally share a moment like this with her sister. She had always thought she would be too worried about Juniper's safety, and she was of course, but it was also special to have her standing right by her side as they discovered the centre of the Lost Desert of Time – together.

'How does it work?' asked Ember.

'Backwards,' said Nick, still gazing at the hourglass. 'You see, each grain of sand helps to track time, but time is infinite. So the hourglass pulls in time from the desert at the bottom and sends it back into the desert once it has been tracked. It's paused at the moment, while you squeeze in your extra minutes. When your time is up, you'll see the sand begin to move again.'

'The very first grain of sand,' Ember wondered aloud. 'Is it in there?'

Nick nodded. 'Of course. But she's in me too. She's

everywhere. Everything here was created from that first grain.'

'Wow,' said Juniper. 'It's . . .'

'Utterly indescribable,' said Hans. Ember and Juniper locked eyes and started to laugh. Hans always chose the most surprising words.

But as they laughed, Ember felt her hourglass begin to disintegrate between her fingers. She held it up and it crumbled, the sand tumbling down to the ground, ready to join the pit. Juniper's did the same.

Inside the enormous hourglass of time, the star-like pieces of sand began to move. As Nick had said it would, rather than falling down, the sand began to rise. Pieces of sand were piled high in the bottom of the glass and slowly, like tiny fireflies, were lifted in a steady stream until they squeezed through the centre of the glass. In the top half, the sand grains drifted up, spiralling higher and higher until they reached the dune's ceiling.

Time had begun again.

As she watched quietly, something became clear in Ember's mind.

'It's impossible,' she whispered. 'If sand travels up,

then the only way to turn back time would be to have the sand travel downwards, and to do that you'd have to turn the whole desert upside-down.'

Nick, who had hopped down from Juniper's arms, looked up at Ember and then back at the hourglass. 'I *think* you're right. I've certainly never heard of a way to do it. But we can't be too sure.'

Ember didn't know whether to laugh or cry. If it *was* impossible, Falcon couldn't turn back eight months, destabilising the entire world. But it also meant they couldn't save the people whose threads had been cut. They would be gone for ever, and Ember wouldn't have a way to catch the Thread-Cutter, whether it really *was* Ms Daylands or someone else. Soon enough, S.E.C.R.E.T. would destroy her memories of Hans, of Mount Never, the Fate Cards . . .

She swallowed, her mouth dry. She couldn't give up all hope, not when they had come so far. Right now, they had to focus on what they *could* do.

'Falcon could be here any moment,' said Ember. She pulled Juniper behind her, safely away from the door and the ledge of the pit. 'Even if he can't turn back time, we need to stop him from doing anything else dangerous.'

'How are we going to do that?' asked Juniper.

Ember's mind was racing. 'Nick, could you stand by the door? Hans, stay in my jacket. When he walks in, Hans and I will grab him and Nick can trip him up. Juniper, you take the maps off him,' she added.

Nick's eyes lit up at being a crucial part of the plan, and he scurried around them, standing by the door in position.

'Everyone, be careful not to fall into that pit,' said Hans cheerfully. 'Because there's no way you're getting up from there!'

Ember nodded. 'Thanks, Ha—'

The door to the sand dune burst open.

21

Falcon rushed through the door.

Ember reached out, missing him, but true to the plan he fell over Nick's tough, armoured body, toppling to Ember's feet – as a second figure shoved him out of the way.

For a split second, Ember was bewildered – until she saw the glinting jewellery in the light of the hourglass.

Haywood Larkin.

'*You?*' she said, her voice filled with confusion.

This didn't make sense. Haywood had taken Falcon in, he had come to Everspring to help them, he was supposed to be *good* . . .

Haywood turned to her, and his face – once cheery and friendly – had contorted with disgust and disappointment.

'I thought you said no one followed you,' he sneered at Falcon, clipping him around the head as he stood.

Ember's mind couldn't keep up. But there, tied to Haywood's waist, were the tubes of the four Fate Mountain maps. She glanced at Falcon and saw a strange look on his face . . . shame? Embarrassment? He *should* feel ashamed.

Traitor, she thought.

Falcon avoided Ember's gaze, looking down at the floor.

'They didn't follow me,' muttered Falcon. 'I don't know how they got here.'

Ember opened her mouth to speak, but Haywood held up his hand.

'I should hardly be surprised that you're here,' he snarled. 'Ember Shadows, the arrogant child who thinks she can manipulate the world to suit her, without any regard for anyone else.'

He shoved Falcon out of the way once more and turned to the hourglass.

'Ah,' he said, 'finally, the centre of the Desert. This *must* be it – the key to controlling time itself.'

Ember glowered, anger boiling in her stomach as she tried to make sense of it all.

'I don't understand . . . you came to *help*

272

Everspring,' she said, her voice catching in the back of her throat. 'Why would you want to control time?'

Haywood smirked. 'You are so naïve, Ember. I didn't come to help; I came for the threads.'

'The – the threads?' Ember's mind was racing, trying to make it all fit together.

It was all Haywood. *Haywood* was the Thread-Cutter.

'But . . . why?' she whispered.

'Because of you!' Haywood yelled. 'You ruined everything! As leader of Overwood I had it all, but the moment you changed the Fate Cards, you stole it from me! Everyone wanted a piece of power, and nobody wanted me in charge any more. They removed me from the palace saying I was a cruel ruler, that I was selfish and they vowed that I'd never rule over anyone again. Well, I showed them, didn't I? I didn't need to be their leader to end their lives.'

Ember's skin prickled as she put the pieces together. The threads that had been cut – they hadn't been random after all. Haywood had deliberately cut the threads of the people who had taken away his power; he had killed them from a distance.

Haywood's eyes were burning with anger. 'Then I met *you*, the selfish child who had changed the cards, and well, finding your thread went straight to the top of my list, followed by Ms Daylands'. Everspring would need a leader, if she was removed. I would step in.' He paused and gave Ember a terrifying smile. 'But then you became useful.'

The last few pieces fell into place in Ember's mind.

Falcon had been spying on her on the mountain, spying for Haywood. That was why he had changed his mind about their plan the moment a letter came back from Haywood.

'Once I heard you were looking for a route to the Desert of Time,' Haywood was saying, 'I realised I didn't have to settle for cutting threads or leading the tiny village of Everspring. If I could get to the desert, I could turn back time and get everything back exactly how it was before, when I was a true leader, when people knew their place . . .'

'You can't!' screamed Juniper. 'It's impossible to turn back time. You'd have to turn the whole desert upside down.'

'She's right!' cried Nick in a moment of bravery. 'I

know everything about this desert! I've been here for many, many years, learning about lost and found time, stitches in time, free time and even wasted time. It's one of the best things about being immune to the passage of time – I've had time to learn *all* the ways it can be controlled.'

He paused and stepped forwards an inch, courage shining from his scales. 'I know I can squeeze more minutes in, share my time-stopping immunity, even loan time! But in all my years, I've never, *ever* heard of a way to turn it back. So, you might as well leave now, you horrible, terrible, awful—'

Haywood simply stamped one foot towards Nick, towering over him, and the frightened pangolin scurried behind Ember to cower beside Juniper. Haywood laughed and turned back to the hourglass.

'I'll find a way,' he said.

'But it's not right—' Ember began.

'Not right?' screamed Haywood. Ember saw Falcon flinch, but he didn't move.

'Let me tell you what's *not right*,' Haywood continued, his voice lower now, more threatening. 'My power being torn away from me when *you* decided you

wanted to play with the fates. *I* should be running
Overwood. *I* should be sitting in the city palace. That
should all still be *mine*. But it was taken from me, all
of it.'

'But you can't—'

Haywood stopped her with a laugh. 'Oh but I can!'
he said. 'Cutting threads was good revenge, but you've
handed me the greatest power of all. *Time.*'

Ember clenched her fists. She opened her mouth to respond, when Falcon stepped forward.

'Ember, Haywood's right,' he said. 'He was given a fate and promised a future, like the people in your village were promised theirs. You took that from them and from us. Don't make the same mistake again.'

Ember shook her head. Had she really taken the futures of all those people? *Moira* had done that, not her.

'But Falcon, *your* life was taken from you, when you were banished, because of the Fate Cards,' said Hans. 'Your family—'

'He has me now,' said Haywood. 'That's all the family he needs. Together we're going to make things right so we both get what we deserve.'

Ember shook her head. 'That's not how things work. None of us are entitled to any part of life, good or bad.' She glared at Haywood. 'How are you planning to make things right, anyway? Because you *can't* turn back time. Even Nick knows it's impossible—'

'Maybe turning back time is impossible,' sneered Haywood, a sudden glint in his eye. 'But there's always a Plan B.'

He looked down at Nick, then at Falcon, and back to Ember.

With one hand, he pushed Ember out of the way, and she stumbled into the side of dune's wall. With his other hand, Haywood reached down and grabbed Nick by the tail. Hanging upside down, Nick began to shoot his tongue out frantically, his scales rippling in panic. Ember clambered to her feet and lunged forward, desperately trying to grab him, but Haywood was too tall.

'This is the difference between you and I, Ember Shadows,' said Haywood. 'I know what I'm entitled to. I know what's right. I might not know how to turn back time, but I can see how to *stop* it.' He was staring at the hourglass in front of them with a gleeful smile on his face.

With Nick still firmly in his grasp, Haywood now turned back to Falcon, who was standing near the edge of the crater.

In one swift movement, he laid his other hand on Falcon's shoulder, and shoved.

Ember froze with shock and locked eyes with Falcon, his face etched with fear and desperation as he teetered on the ledge.

He stretched his arms out towards Ember.

But it was too late.

22

Ember watched in horror as Falcon fell, sliding and rolling, tumbling down to the bottom of the crater.

'No!' screamed Juniper.

Falcon clawed hopelessly at the sand, trying not to get pulled under, but Haywood wasn't even watching.

'I don't need to turn back time,' said Haywood. 'All I need to do is stop it. With the world frozen until I'm ready to start it again, I can collect every last thread on every Fate Mountain. With everyone in the world as my hostage, no one will dare take away my power again.'

Ember watched in horror as Falcon's head disappeared beneath the surface. Why had Haywood done this? Then she understood.

Haywood was using his own apprentice to block the hourglass.

'Although I'll make an exception for you two,' snarled Haywood to Ember and Juniper. 'I won't keep *your* threads. I think I might cut both of yours up as soon as I find them. Maybe even Falcon's too.'

'Don't you dare touch those children's threads!' cried Nick, trying to break free from Haywood's grip. 'Now, let me go!'

Nick thrashed desperately from side to side as Haywood wrestled him into a stronghold, pulled the rope from his belt and began to tie it around Nick, lashing him to his own shoulders so he couldn't move.

As he did, Ember had an idea.

'Hans,' she whispered. 'Can you stand on my shoulder? And get ready to stay extremely still in a second.'

Hans nodded, puzzled, and hopped up on to Ember's shoulder, while Ember turned back to the hourglass. Falcon's head had just burst through the sand inside the bottom half of the hourglass. He was panting, out of breath, as his body floated up with the sand, his arms and legs desperately flailing as he reached for the side of the hourglass.

'Help! Help! Haywood, help me!' But Haywood didn't even acknowledge Falcon's muffled cries.

'We have to *do* something!' screamed Juniper,

pushing past Ember to get to the hourglass.

Ember held her back and looked her deep in the eyes. 'Trust me,' she whispered. 'It's the only way.'

Together, they watched as Falcon floated higher and higher until, eventually, he was just inches from the middle of the hourglass. She had hated him for betraying her, but this, this was too much to bear.

With Nick secure, Haywood turned to watch. 'Time to say goodbye to your freedom,' he whispered, sneering.

Falcon hit the hourglass' funnel and froze in place, his eyes staring wide at Ember, his back blocking the funnel as the sand rose from the bottom.

'No!' shouted Juniper. But as she reached forwards, the grains of time stopped floating, and Juniper froze in place, with her arm outstretched towards Falcon's rigid body.

Haywood had done it.

Ember stood perfectly still on the edge of the crater, her eyes still on Falcon; Hans stood on her shoulder like a freeze frame.

Next to her, Haywood moved freely, thanks to being in contact with Nick.

'Ha ha!' he shouted. 'It worked!'

He stepped forwards, leaning so close that Ember could feel his breath on her face. 'Maybe I won't cut your thread right away. Then you'll be able to see what fun I'm having with everyone else as hostage.'

Haywood straightened up.

'You know, if you'd kept your nose out,' he continued, 'I might never have learnt about the desert at all. I suppose I should *thank* you, Ember Shadows.'

With that, he turned, Nick still twisting in his binding on Haywood's shoulders, and ran out of the dune door.

All around Ember, time had stopped.

Except, of course, for a pair of fidgety feet on her shoulder . . .

'Can I move yet?' whispered Hans.

Finally, Ember shifted. 'Yes, but don't let go of me!' she said, and Hans carefully climbed into her hands.

Ember turned to Juniper, whose arm was stretched out towards the hourglass and Falcon, panic in her eyes. She put a hand on Juniper's shoulder and squeezed gently.

'I'm sorry, Juniper,' she whispered.

Together, Ember and Hans sank to the ground.

'I can't believe he actually did it,' Ember continued. 'And he took Nick. Poor Nick, he must be so scared.'

'Do you think Haywood will . . . will hurt him?' asked Hans.

Ember shook her head. 'He needs Nick like I need you, or he'll get frozen in time. But he will be able to get to the threads.' Ember bit her lip. 'The spiders won't be frozen . . . I hope he doesn't hurt them.'

Silence hung in the air as they stared out at Falcon, trapped in the enormous hourglass.

'We should have let S.E.C.R.E.T. take the memories

in the first place,' whispered Hans. 'Then none of this would have happened.'

Ember chewed the inside of her cheek and said nothing.

'It was selfish of us to think our friendship was important enough to risk all of this,' continued Hans.

Ember looked down at him. With Hans, who was always so happy, it was easy to forget that he was struggling with his own problems beneath the surface. But he was. In fact, *everybody* was. Juniper had been feeling wrapped in cotton wool; Falcon had desperately been searching for acceptance; and even Ember had been wrestling with doubts about whether destroying the Fate Cards had been the right thing to do.

She had spent so long worrying about whether she was making all the right decisions and regretting all the problems she had caused. But now, looking at her best friend, it all seemed so clear.

'Hans, I think you're wrong,' she said. 'I think friendship *is* important enough to risk it all for. Maybe other people would disagree, but that's the thing: we all have to do what *we* believe is right, no matter what anyone else around us is saying.'

She looked over at Falcon, then at Juniper.

'I don't regret going up Mount Never to save Juniper, and I don't regret taking down Moira,' she said, feeling the weight of it lift from her chest. 'We can't change what has already happened, not our own actions, or someone else's. We can only learn from them.'

Ember blinked back tears of anger. More than anything, she wished she could undo the awful things Haywood had done and save his victims from the terrible fate of a cut thread.

But she knew with all her heart now that it was done. No matter how much she hated what had happened, they could only move forwards.

Looking down at Hans sitting on her lap, she squeezed his hands. 'I don't regret coming on this adventure either. Our friendship is worth the risk to me, and, if I believe it to be right, then I have to be confident in what I choose, and carry on. None of us can live doing what someone else believes to be right – look where that's got Falcon.'

Hans blinked, and a puzzled look came over his face. 'You really think our friendship is that important?'

'Of course I do,' Ember said. 'No matter what the risk, I would never let someone take my memories of you away without a fight. We're more than friends; you're part of my family now.'

Hans beamed from one side of his face to the other.

'I've never had a family before!' he said. 'Now I have *two* sisters! That's double-perfect.' He paused, and then his eyes opened wide. 'Does that mean . . .' he began sheepishly, 'that I'm Hans *Shadows*?'

Ember smiled. 'If you want to be,' she said.

Hans broke into a delighted dance for a moment, but quickly stopped as he saw Ember's sombre face.

'Unfortunately,' said Ember, 'none of that solves our current problem.'

She looked over at Falcon. There was no way they could turn back time and save Haywood's victims. Which meant there was also no way to protect their memories from S.E.C.R.E.T.'s plan. At least while time was stopped for the whole world, Ember knew her memories would be safe.

The only thing they could do now was stop Haywood from stealing the threads. Hans watched as her mind ticked into action. 'Ember Shadows,' Hans said with a grin. 'Do you have a plan?'

And, with confidence building inside her, Ember grinned back.

23

Careful never to break contact, Hans sat on Ember's shoulder and held on to her ear and neck. It tickled Ember, but she had bigger things to think about.

She held Juniper's hand gently – her body was so stiff, she didn't want to risk breaking a finger.

'We'll be back, Juniper, I promise,' she said. 'We're going to stop Haywood and then I'll come back and fix all of this.'

Hans reached out and touched Juniper too. 'Don't worry, Juniper Shadows. We'll be back. Never leave a Shadows behind!'

With one final look back at Falcon and Juniper, Ember hurried towards the dune's door.

Slowly, as slowly as she could manage, she pulled it open and peered around the outside.

There was no way Haywood would have made it out of the Desert of Time yet, and she had a sneaky suspicion Nick would be making it as difficult as possible for him. So Ember needed to stay hidden, because if Haywood realised she hadn't been paused with the rest of the world, there would be trouble.

Her plan was risky. In fact, it was much more than risky.

She was relying on Haywood not going to Mount Never first. If he did, then everything was lost.

She crept out of the door and looked around for Haywood. She couldn't see him anywhere.

Now was another risky part. She needed to get to Mount Never herself, which was straight ahead. She'd have to sprint through the desert to get to the tunnel entrance without being seen. Ember assumed the other mountains were accessed from other parts of the desert, but she didn't know where.

'Ready?' she said to Hans. 'I'm going to run as fast as I possibly can.'

Hans nodded and clung tightly to her, digging his fingers into her hair.

Then, Ember began to sprint. The sand slipped beneath her feet and her legs felt like jelly, but she kept going, racing forward as fast as she could. She made it to the Time Bank where she had met Nick, and kept running on and on until she came to the centre of the desert clearing. Ahead, she could see the tunnel to Mount Never.

Suddenly, she heard a voice.

'Don't you understand, you stupid pangolin?' It was Haywood, from somewhere close by. Ember dropped to the sand and lay flat on her stomach, not daring to look up. Hans clung tight to her hair. She shuffled in the sand as silently as she could, desperately trying to cover her body.

Then, as if the desert itself wanted to help, a breeze pulled a gust of sand towards her, covering them both.

'You can slow me down as much as you like,' continued Haywood. 'But this is going to happen whether you co-operate or not. The only way it will be better for you is if you help me.'

'I won't ever co-operate with you!' Nick shrieked.

'You want to be careful,' said Haywood. 'As soon as I've collected the threads, I won't need you any more. You saw what happens to people when I stop needing them.'

Ember heard Nick gasp.

Had he spotted her? She could tell they were close by. *Please don't let Haywood look this way*, she pleaded silently.

'Fine,' stammered Nick. 'The closest entrance is the one to Mount When. It's over there, to the west of the dune.'

'Good pangolin,' said Haywood patronisingly. 'That's better.'

She heard the footsteps move further and further away until they disappeared completely. Despite the situation, Ember smiled a little. 'Nick is trying to slow Haywood down,' she told Hans. 'The entrance to Mount Never must be closer than the one to When, it's right here!'

After checking the coast was clear, Ember ran past the Lost and Found towards the opening of the tunnel to Mount Never. As she stepped inside, she stopped, remembering her sister frozen in time.

'Juniper will be safe, for now,' said Hans.

Ember nodded, and they hurried into the darkness.

*

When they reached Mount Never, it was chaos.

The Threads of Fate still inside the mountain were

frozen, which meant those outside on the mountain would be too.

The spiders were free to move around, and by the looks of it, they were terrified.

Scurrying about in a frenzy, the spiders were wailing, shouting, and hysterical.

'Lacey!' Ember shouted, spotting her in a small huddle of spiders. 'Lacey!'

Lacy turned and Ember swallowed. Lacey was clearly *furious*.

Her eight eyes set upon Ember, and, before Ember even had a chance to speak, Lacey had scuttled right in front of her.

'You!' she screamed, and the whole mountain fell immediately silent. 'We trusted you and now time has stopped! Our one duty in life is to protect time and because of you, we failed.'

'I know,' Ember said, full of apology. 'And I'm sorry.'

'Sorry? Is that it?'

'No,' said Ember. 'I know how we can catch the person responsible. But I need your help again.'

'Our help!?' Lacey looked as though she would

explode with rage. 'HELP?'

'A man called Haywood is the one who stopped time and he's coming to take the threads. He's incredibly clever and determined. You have to help me, or everyone is in danger,' Ember pleaded.

'Please,' Hans urged from Ember's shoulder. 'Our sister is stuck in the Desert of Time and once Haywood doesn't need time to be frozen any more, she'll be in a lot of danger.'

'Juniper's stuck?' A spider's voice broke through the crowd as he hurried forward.

Juniper . . . Juniper . . . Everywhere, Juniper's name rippled through the spiders. It seemed she had left a mark on them all.

Lacey's face softened a bit. 'Is she OK?'

'She is right now,' Ember said. 'But if we don't catch Haywood, who knows what he'll do to her. We have to catch him, and then I'll be able to start the hourglass again and free Juniper.' A hoard of blank spider faces stared back at her. 'I know it doesn't make much sense. All I can ask is that you do what you truly believe to be the right thing.'

Lacey regarded Ember for what felt like a long

time, then finally, she sighed, her whole spider body heaving with the air. 'Fine. For Juniper.'

Ember felt her shoulders relax slightly, grateful once again for her sister's kindness towards animals.

'OK, here's the plan.'

*

Once they were ready, Ember walked into the tunnel with Hans on her shoulder, and they waited, hiding under the cover of darkness.

It felt as though they were waiting for hours, but how long it had truly been was impossible to say, especially as time had stopped . . . everything felt complicated.

'Are you OK?' Ember asked.

Hans nodded and gave her head a gentle pat. 'I only hope we can catch Haywood, free Falcon and Juniper, return any Threads of Fate that Haywood has taken to the mountains where they belong, get back to S.E.C.R.E.T. HQ before Anise reaches Cloud Memory, *and* somehow persuade them not to wipe the memories after all.'

They still had so much to do, and every part of their plan relied on the part before it going smoothly.

Ember closed her eyes for a moment, until she heard a voice that made her whole body tense up. Part one of the plan was about to begin, it seemed.

'Two mountains down, two to go.'

Haywood had entered the tunnel.

'Please,' cried Nick. 'Two is more than enough. You don't need everyone's threads – that's too much power!'

'Shut up and stop squirming,' demanded Haywood.

Ember held her breath. Hans dug his hands deep into her hair so they wouldn't lose contact with one another. Carefully, Ember reached down to the ground and grabbed a handful of sand. With the other hand, she held the teacup that the mon-keys in the Tremoring Tropics had given her.

Then, she dropped the sand into the cup.

It began to vibrate, the storm inside brewing and bubbling, trembling with the added ingredient.

Ember waited patiently until Haywood's footsteps were so loud that she was sure he was only metres ahead of her. Drawing on every ounce of courage inside of her, she shook the Illumitube around her neck.

The glow flooded the tunnel around them.

And, as Haywood met her gaze, his face a picture of shock and surprise, she pulled the teacup's handle.

24

The moment right after Ember pulled the handle seemed to last for ever.

Haywood's eyes burned brightly in the glow of her Illumitube, and she didn't dare look away.

He was clutching a red bag Ember knew must be filled with hundreds, if not thousands, of frozen Threads of Fate.

As he lifted his foot to step towards her, the storm burst from the teacup.

It was as though she had released a volcanic eruption from the palm of her hand. A tornado of sand shot from the cup, widening as it reached towards the ceiling. Ember hoped with every bone in her body that mixing sand in with the storm had worked the way she wanted it to. They would need more than a simple storm to slow down Haywood. They needed a *sandstorm*.

As the spiral of sand rose, claps of thunder bellowed

louder and louder, until the sand tornado smashed into the ceiling of the tunnel, and Ember knew they had to run.

She dropped the teacup to the floor, the shattering barely audible amid the crashing of the storm around them.

With Hans clinging to her shoulder, Ember began sprinting towards Mount Never.

She could feel the sandstorm chasing them, the heat of it against her neck, sharp pieces of sand spraying up towards them as they ran. The thunder echoed around them, bouncing off the sides of the tunnel, but still she kept on running, wishing now she hadn't come so far into the tunnel.

'EMBER!' a voice behind her screamed. *Was it Nick?* Ember hoped he was OK.

Suddenly, a bright fork of lightning crashed past her ear, sending her stumbling to the ground. As she rose, she saw with horror that the storm was gaining on them.

Plumes of sand were racing through the tunnel like waves in an ocean, contorted into the shape of storm clouds. Maybe she had gone too far. Maybe a simple storm would have been enough . . .

But there was no time to worry. Hans tugged on her hair in fear, and she began to run again, sprinting back to the mountain as another bolt of lightning narrowly missed her left foot. Ahead, she could see the spiders at the end of the tunnel.

They weren't far; they were going to make it. Ember raced on, her legs wobbly beneath her until finally, she was there. She leapt out of the tunnel's mouth and darted to the side, pressing her back against the mountain wall. In perfect synchronisation, the swarm of spiders moved forwards, pulling a web over the mouth of the tunnel.

'The threads! Haywood's got them! Someone needs to get the threads!' Ember shouted.

But at that moment, the sandstorm thundered through into the centre of the mountain. Only just safe from its reaches, Ember stood and watched helplessly as the clouds billowed around the spiders at the tunnel's entrance. But then, when she was worried they might all be blown away, the storm began to weaken and it retreated into the same tornado shape that had first emerged from the teacup.

With a grumble of thunder, the storm shot upwards and exploded into a light mist.

As Ember looked at the mouth of the tunnel, she thought she might scream with delight.

Haywood was stuck to an enormous web, arms and legs flailing as he struggled with the binds the spiders had put on him. Lacey stood close by, holding Haywood's bag, containing the Threads of Fate from the other mountains.

Nick was still strapped to Haywood's shoulders with the rope, his tail thrashing round helplessly. But at least he was safe now.

'Get me out of here!' Haywood screamed in fury.

But the spiders weren't about to let him free. Instead, they were wrapping him in a cocoon of webbing. Ember knew there was no way he'd *ever* get out of that.

She stepped towards him.

'Nick, we'll have you out of there in a moment, OK?' said Ember, pushing her fingers through the web to touch him. He met her finger with his tongue, and Ember smiled, despite the slobber.

'We did it, we did it, ooh la la, we did it,' said Hans, dancing on her shoulder, with one hand still buried in her hair.

The spiders rolled Haywood on to the floor, and to Ember's surprise, she noticed he was smirking. He appeared to be horribly pleased with himself.

And then, with a sinking feeling in her stomach, Ember saw why.

In his hand, he held a single Thread of Fate. In the other hand he held his short knife, glinting in the light.

'I suggest you get me out of here right now,' said Haywood. 'Or this thread gets cut.'

Every spider in the mountain seemed to hold their breath. Hans held Ember even closer; she could feel him against her ear.

'Don't free him!' shouted Nick. 'It's only one thread! We have to re-start time, and all the others are safe!'

But Lacey rushed forwards. 'Not in a million years,' she roared. 'Every thread is precious; that's a human life!'

Haywood held Ember's gaze, his eyes glinting with triumph.

'We can't let him, can we, Ember?' whispered Hans.

It was one life, in exchange for all the others; and yet, still Ember knew in her heart she couldn't let that thread be damaged.

She shook her head. 'Let him out,' she muttered.

'But, Ember!' called Nick.

'Are you sure about this?' said Hans. 'Are we making the right decision?'

She pulled him into her hands and looked at him carefully. 'We decided, didn't we? Always do what you think is the right thing. No matter what.'

Hans nodded.

'So, what do you think?' Ember asked.

'We can't let any thread be cut. Not a single one,' said Hans.

Ember smiled sadly. 'I agree.'

The spiders pulled the web from Haywood, and he staggered to his feet, still clinging to his hostage thread. Lacey's leg clutched the bag with the rest of the threads tighter, and Haywood stepped forwards.

'Now, give me that bag, and let me go and collect *this* mountain's threads,' he said. 'Or else.' He waved his knife in front of Lacey's face.

With a look at Ember, Lacey let the bag go. Haywood snatched it from her grip, and Ember's blood began to boil.

She couldn't let him take all the threads! She had to come up with a plan! But the cogs in her mind couldn't turn fast enough. There was no time to think it over, to invent something to help, or to worry whether or not she would fail. So she did the only thing she could think to do: in one quick swoop, she jumped on to Haywood's back like a treebear, and began tugging at the rope that was keeping Nick attached to him. Hans reached out from her jacket to help, one hand on Ember's neck, one hand working around the knots that were keeping Nick prisoner.

Haywood spun around, confused and helpless, and as he reached for Ember, he dropped the bag, threads spilling all around him. 'No!' he screamed. 'Stop it! You can't—'

Ember loosened the second knot, and Nick leapt free from his shoulders.

Haywood froze in place, his face filled with anger and panic, arms rigid and twisted where he had been reaching to pull Ember from his back.

For a moment, there was silence.

Then, an almighty cheer erupted around them, thousands of spiders whooping and yelling in celebration.

They had got him!

Hans squealed. 'HA HA, HAYWOOD!' he yelled. 'Time for *you* to say goodbye to your freedom! You mean, silly, horrible—'

'Come on, Hans,' interrupted Ember, breathless. 'We've still got to get Falcon and Juniper.'

Lacey held out a leg to stop her. 'Thank you,' she said.

'We couldn't have done it without your help,' said Ember. 'Thank *you*.'

'Leave the criminal to us and we'll make sure he's here when you get back,' Lacey said. 'Is there anything else we can do to help?'

'Actually,' said Ember, an idea coming to mind, 'we might need some of your web-thread.'

*

Ember, Nick and Hans pushed open the door to the dune to find everything just as they had left it. Juniper was still frozen, and Falcon was still trapped in the hourglass.

'OK, do we all know our roles?' asked Ember.

Hans and Nick nodded from her shoulders, and she wrapped Lacey's thread around her waist, tying it carefully. Then, she dug her feet deep into the sand until most of her calves were covered.

Once Nick had a good grip of Ember's shoulder, Hans leapt down to the ground. Ember tied the other end of the thread around Hans, making sure it was tight enough that it wouldn't come free over his turned-out feet or wide, pointed head.

'Ready?' she asked.

'Definitely.' He leapt into the air before looping down and charging right to the bottom of the crater. Ember felt the thread travel through her hands; she was glad Lacey had given them so much. She kept her eyes trained on Hans, watching as his metallic skin glinted in the light of the hourglass. Once he had reached the bottom of the crater, he dived into the sand and right under the glass. Soon enough, he popped up inside the hourglass, and leapt into the air with as much energy as she had ever seen. Pinging himself off the wall of glass, he bounced his way to Falcon.

'Now loop the thread around him!' Ember shouted.

Hans made a salute and began to wrap the thread all the way around Falcon's middle. Then, he turned to Ember, and gave a thumbs up sign.

Ember looked at Nick. 'Please don't let go,' she said. 'If you let go, I'll be stuck in time too, and then we'll have a real pro—'

'Yes, yes, I know how it works,' Nick said. 'If I remember rightly, *I* told *you* the rules.'

Ember smiled and began to pull. As Ember heaved, the sands around Falcon began to tremble.

Bit by bit, the thread tightened, until, with one final pull, Falcon came away from the hourglass' middle.

Finally, a single grain of sand passed around Falcon from the bottom of the hourglass, through the funnel, to the top, and Falcon's body unfroze.

'FALCON!' screamed Juniper, coming to life.

Ember nearly jumped out of her skin before bursting into laughter at her sister's confused face.

'What happened?' Juniper asked. 'How did you get— Where's Haywood? Why are you—'

Ember shook her head and giggled. 'Come and help me,' she said. 'I'll explain later.'

Together, they pulled Hans and Falcon all the way out of the crater, helping them back over the edge. Falcon scrambled to his feet and, for a moment, no one said anything.

'I, I—' started Falcon, looking Ember directly in the eye. 'I'm really sorry. I thought he was . . .' Falcon looked at Juniper and Hans, then back at Ember. 'I thought he was my new family.'

'Well, it turned out he was an . . .'

'OLD FART!' shouted Hans gleefully, before snorting with laughter.

Juniper, who never seemed to stop surprising Ember, reached out a hand to Falcon. 'We can be your family for now, if you like? At least until we help you find your twin sister.'

Falcon smiled down at her, and then looked at Ember. 'Thanks for not leaving me there,' he said. 'Guess you're not *so* bad.'

Ember rolled her eyes. 'I didn't do it for *you*,' she said. 'We just didn't want you stopping time for ever.'

'That's not true,' said Hans. 'You said we had to save Juniper *and* Falcon. We like Falcon, don't we?'

Ember gave Falcon a grudging smile. 'He's all right, I suppose,' she said. 'Let's go home, shall we?' She turned to Nick. 'Are you coming with us too?'

Nick's eyes widened in disbelief. 'Are you *joking*? Do you have any idea how much cataloguing of lost time I have to do now?'

'I didn't think of that!' said Ember. 'Don't forget to take our time we owe you from earlier.'

'Oh don't worry,' said Nick, ushering them out of the door to the dune. 'I won't.'

With that, he slammed the door, leaving Ember, Juniper, Falcon and Hans to return to Mount Never.

The others started forwards, but Ember hung back, a lump in her throat.

'What's wrong?' said Hans, turning to her.

Ember blinked, trying to hold back a sudden urge to cry. 'We couldn't turn back time, so we couldn't save the Thread-Cutter's victims. And . . .'

She took a deep breath, almost unable to say it out loud. 'Time's started again. Any minute, Anise and the rest of S.E.C.R.E.T. are going to wipe our memories.'

'I know,' said Hans. 'But I realised something. If time doesn't affect me, I don't think Cloud Memory will either. So, they can't wipe *my* memories. And you and Juniper are *family*. I'll tell you all our stories, and after a while, things will be OK. We'll be friends again.'

'You really think so?' asked Ember. 'You'd work that hard to start our friendship all over again?'

'Of course I would!' he said, and leapt into the air, on to her shoulder. 'It's the most important thing in the world to me. Now, let's go home.'

25

When they reached Mount Never, Ember couldn't quite believe the sight ahead of her.

Haywood was sitting, legs crossed, in the middle of the mountain, surrounded by a group of spiders acting guard. They were hardly needed though; his hands were bound tightly with web, his mouth covered by it, and his legs had been wound in so much there was no way he'd be able to even stand.

Behind him, having what looked like a *very* important discussion, were Jasper, Anise, May, and another man they hadn't seen before.

S.E.C.R.E.T. agents? In Mount Never?

They were in real trouble now.

'I'm sorry,' said Ember, hurrying ahead of the rest. 'It was all my fault. Again.'

Jasper turned to her and raised an eyebrow curiously. 'It was?'

Ember nodded. 'But . . .' She paused. 'To be honest,

I'd do it all over again. I still don't believe you should wipe anyone's memories, and I'll *never* be sorry for saving Juniper and exposing Moira. I'm only sorry I caused you all such problems.'

She took a deep breath and relaxed a little. It felt right to stick to her convictions and be proud of her choice, even if they didn't agree with it.

'And you?' said Jasper, peering round Ember to look at Falcon. 'What have you got to say for yourself?'

Falcon stepped forwards to join Ember. 'I'm sorry, and . . . well, I *do* regret trusting Haywood. I just wanted to belong somewhere.'

Ember glanced quickly at May, but even she didn't offer a smile.

Then Ember had a thought. 'Anise, why aren't you on your way to Cloud Memory?'

As if by magic, all four of the S.E.C.R.E.T. agents broke into grins.

'I made it all the way there,' explained Anise excitedly. 'I even got as far as setting up the machine to wipe memories – when suddenly a new memory appeared in your bank.'

Ember frowned, intrigued.

'I could see the memory of what you'd done – saving Falcon, catching Haywood, rescuing the threads,' Anise said. 'It was all there in your memory bank.'

'Anise hurried back to tell me what she'd seen and we came here right away,' said Jasper. 'You see, we need more people like you around. If we got rid of your memories, well, you'd be pretty useless to us I think.'

Ember blushed, not sure if she was still in trouble or if that was actually a compliment. 'But . . . I couldn't turn back time. I couldn't save the people Haywood killed.'

'No, but you caught him and saved every single thread on every Fate Mountain,' said Anise. 'You stopped any future harm *without* needing to destroy any memories. We could hardly let you forget that.'

'Right,' said Jasper gravely. 'Now we have a very important question to ask Falcon and Juniper.'

Falcon and Juniper exchanged a worried glance, and then looked up at Jasper.

'We were wondering if you would like to start as apprentices at S.E.C.R.E.T.?' he said with a smile. 'We could do with a couple of brave agents like you two.'

May beamed at Falcon. 'I was thinking you could do your apprenticeship with me? We all make mistakes, and I've seen first-hand how much potential kindness you have.'

'Yes!' said Falcon. 'That would be fantastic! Thank you so much.'

'And Juniper,' said Jasper, 'this is Topaz Blackthorne, assigned to the Tremoring Tropics.'

Topaz stepped forwards. He was tall and wearing a long green trench coat. His eyes shone like the gem he had been named after. He studied Juniper for a moment and reached out his hand to shake hers.

'I hear you've got a way with animals,' he said. 'That would be most useful in our line of work. So, what do you think? Can I count on you to be my apprentice?'

'Really?' asked Juniper, shaking his hand. 'That would be . . .'

'Utterly indescribable?' asked Hans with a squeal.

'Exactly,' said Juniper, and Ember couldn't have felt prouder of her little sister.

'Now, Ember Shadows and Hans—' began Jasper.

'Hans Shadows,' interrupted Ember. 'He's one of the Shadows *siblings*.'

Ember took a sideways look at Hans; he looked as though he might explode with joy.

'Is that so?' said Jasper. 'Well, we're terribly sorry, but there simply aren't enough apprenticeships for all of you.'

Ember felt a pit open in her stomach, and tried to close it quickly. It didn't matter. Yes, she would have loved to be an apprentice – but Juniper and Falcon were safe and had exciting positions, and she was just happy to not be in trouble any more. 'That's OK,' she said, trying to force a smile.

'It is?' asked Jasper as he leaned on his cane. 'Good, because we rather hoped you'd both work together as agents here – and on the other Fate Mountains. You've already saved them *twice*. In fact, you're doing a much better job than we've done for generations. We need someone to make sure that there are no other Moiras or Haywoods trying to take control of the mountains for their own gain . . .'

Before Ember had chance to respond, Hans had shot off her shoulder and into the air, whooping and cheering around them. After a few more whirls and twirls of celebration, he landed, out of breath, right next to her.

'Is that a yes?' asked Jasper. 'After some training, of course.'

'It's an absolutely-stupendipity-YES!' screamed Hans.

'It's a yes!' said Ember.

'Good, now let's all get back to Everspring,' said Jasper. 'Topaz will deal with Haywood. I think your Ms Daylands deserves an update on everything that's happened . . .'

*

When the next village meeting began, Ember was ready, standing at the front with Ms Daylands.

Hundreds were packed into the Council Hut this time, but Ember didn't wish the ground would swallow her up. Instead, she stood proudly.

As she waited, Ember scanned the room for familiar faces. Flint, standing at the back wearing his grey overalls and hat, gave her a wave. On his shoulder sat Florence, notebook in wing, ready to take notes. Her feathery friend gave her a quick wink. Then, of course, there were Juniper, Hans and Falcon in the front row, and her mum sitting proudly beside their funny little family.

Ms Daylands clapped loudly and settled the crowd. 'Ember has agreed to say a few words, but I do want to speak first. I owe all of you an explanation. I know that my absences from Everspring have not gone unnoticed. But I'm pleased to say they have paid off.' She paused and took a deep breath. 'I have been learning as much as I can about the Threads of Fate and how they can be manipulated. I have also cobbled together pieces from the Fate Machine which Moira used to control our lives for decades. I hope that, by seeing it and understanding how it worked, you'll be able to see why we are better off without the Fate Cards.'

A rumble of muttering swept through the crowd.

Ms Daylands paused, looking around the room. 'Also,' she continued, 'a dear new friend of mine, Oaken Swallowson, will be visiting Everspring this week to help us consider how we wish to live our lives. He's a little . . . eccentric. But he has lived his whole life without the cards, and I think we could do with hearing from someone like that now. I believe that with a little help, we can all look forward to a bright future – of our own making.' She turned to Ember. 'Over to you.'

Ember took a deep breath.

'I am here to say sorry,' she announced to the room. 'But not for stopping Moira.'

There were gasps around the room.

'I made a decision that affected everybody, and I truly believe it was the right decision. But I didn't help figure out what would happen after everything changed. So now, I want to help as much as I can. I don't have all the answers, but I think if we work together, we can find them.'

She took another deep breath. 'Ms Daylands and I thought we could use today to start sharing advice about how we could best live without the cards. *My* advice is to live as you believe in your heart to be right. If you can do that, then you're off to a good start.'

She looked down at Falcon. 'You'll make some mistakes along the way, but it's impossible to go back and change what happened. So, we've got to be open to changing our minds too.

'Most of all, you've got to believe in yourself, no matter what. Because you can choose who to be now. So, make it someone good.'

It started at the back of the room, and, slowly, applause started to spread across the hall.

Phew, thought Ember.

Mum smiled proudly back at her, clapping as she did.

Ms Daylands gave her a pat on the shoulder. 'Well said, dear. Now, let's break off into groups and get started!'

Once the groups were talking amongst themselves, sharing advice and ideas, and Ember had returned to her family, Falcon nudged her in the ribs. For a second, she thought he was going to comment on her speech, but instead she realised he was holding up his watch for her to see. A tiny little bell shape in the middle was vibrating.

'S.E.C.R.E.T. needs us,' he whispered.

Ember nodded, made eye contact with Juniper and Hans, and gestured for them to leave.

'Sorry, Mum,' she said, giving her a quick kiss on the cheek.

'You've got nothing to apologise for,' her mother said. 'Dad would be so proud of you, of *all* of you. Now go protect those mountains.'

Ember hurried outside where Falcon was waiting.

'A message is coming through from them now,' he

said. 'Hold on a second.'

As they waited anxiously, Ember looked up at Mount Never. There, the Fateweaver's house still loomed over them. But it was no longer seesawing wildly. It still tipped back and forth a little, but Ember believed it would settle, eventually.

'I don't believe it,' whispered Falcon. He looked up at Ember, then to Juniper and Hans, his eyes wide. 'I might need to use May's bravery already. I think we've got our first mission!'

Excitement buzzed between the four friends.

Magical landscapes, a secret society, and their first mission . . .

Ember wondered what adventures were in store for them this time.

ACKNOWLEDGEMENTS

Writing not just one adventure, but a whole series of stories with Ember and her friends was something that a few years ago I hadn't even considered a possibility. And so my first thanks must go to two people who saw more in Ember right from the start. To Kate Shaw, my amazing agent, who continues to believe in me and my work more than I could ever hope for. And to my incredible editor, Lena McCauley, who imagined the wider world beyond the first book before even I could, and who helped shape the story into the adventure it is today.

It's an ongoing dream to work with the talented team at Hachette Children's Group. Thank you to Samuel Perrett for creating another wonderfully designed book that sits so perfectly with the first. Thank you to illustrator Raquel Ochoa who has once again brought to life Ember and her friends so brilliantly. I never tire of seeing Hans' little face! To Lucy Clayton and Anna Cole, for all their hard work in getting Ember into the hands of readers, and for taking me on my first signings and school events. Thanks to Krissi Hill and Beth McWilliams for their endless creativity, stunning assets and ongoing support. Thank you also to desk editor Ruth Girmatsion, copy editor Genevieve Herr, proofreader Becca Allen and to Ronnie McMahon in production. It never fails to amaze me just how many people there are behind a book; thank you also to the wonderful sales and rights teams who have worked so hard to get Ember's story into readers' hands as far and wide as possible.

Thank you to all the authors who offered such kind words about Ember and her adventure, as well as the book bloggers, early readers and supporters who have been so generous in their reviews. Thanks also to the amazing schools who have welcomed me, and the incredible children who have embraced Ember and all the strangeness of her world. And of course the booksellers, who have welcomed me for events, supported school visits and recommended Ember Shadows to their customers. To my fabulous writer friends, Heather, Kate, Natasha and Rachael, thank you for being an ongoing source of support.